That's a Keeper

Books by

H. Norman Wright

FROM BETHANY HOUSE PUBLISHERS

The Complete Book of Christian Wedding Vows

The Perfect Catch

That's a Keeper

H. NORMAN WRIGHT

REFLECTIONS ON LIFE FROM A
BASS FISHERMAN

That's a Keeper

Illustrated by Sheryl Macauley

BETHANYHOUSE
PUBLISHERS
MINNEAPOLIS, MINNESOTA

Published by Bethany House Publishers
A Ministry of Bethany Fellowship International
11400 Hampshire Avenue South
Bloomington, Minnesota 55438
www.bethanyhouse.com

Printed in the United States of America

Library of Congress Cataloging-in-Publication Data

Wright, H. Norman.
    That's a keeper : reflections on life from a bass fisherman / by H. Norman Wright ; illustrated by Sheryl Macauley.
        p. cm.
    ISBN 0-7642-2550-2 (alk. paper)
    1. Fishing—Religious aspects—Christianity. 2. Fishers—Religious life. I. Title.
    BV4596.F5 W76 2002
    242'.68—dc21

                                                            2002000974

H. NORMAN WRIGHT is an avid bass fisherman and the author of more than sixty books. He is a licensed Marriage, Family, and Child therapist and is the founder and director of Christian Marriage Enrichment. Norm's largest bass to date topped out at ten pounds, one ounce. He and his wife, Joyce, make their home in Long Beach, California.

SHERYL MACAULEY is an award-winning artist who specializes in creating miniature paintings on fingernails. With Norm Wright as her father, it's no surprise that she was introduced to fishing at the early age of four. Indeed, her first drawing ever was of a fish. Sheryl's largest catch to date is a 22-pound northern pike. She, her husband, Bill, and their daughter live in Bakersfield, California.

Contents

That's a Keeper

*Y*our child catches her first fish. And that's a keeper. Of course it is! Anyone's first is a keeper. Wasn't yours? It didn't matter the size or color or species. I've known some people to take the first one home and save it in the freezer for years. It's special. It's only after we've been fishing a while that selectivity and pickiness set in and size dictates our selection.

Before the advent of the new fish mounts, great care was taken in wrapping and freezing that keeper so it would arrive at the taxidermist intact. Patiently we'd wait, often for several months, before that mount would be ready. And when it was, we'd let everyone know about it.

My first keeper mount wasn't really intentional. Have you ever made an off-the-cuff, thoughtless comment to your kids just to placate them and get them to mellow out? And then it backfires? You may know the feeling.

Before I discovered the joy of bass angling, trout was a mainstay. In the early '70s we were fishing at Jenny Lake in Grand Teton National Park. Sheryl, my daughter, was ten or eleven and was constantly asking me when I was going to get a fish mounted. One morning as we walked through the forest to the inlet she started in again, and to settle this (and make sure I wouldn't have to fork out any money for a mount) I said, "Okay, when I catch a Yellowstone cutthroat over twenty inches, I'll do it." She was satisfied, and I was smug . . . until an hour later when I held up a brilliant-colored twenty-one-inch cutt. Sheryl was ecstatic. I have to admit I was excited too, but a bit poorer. It was worth the cost. It really was a keeper.

Sheryl caught a keeper twenty years later. We took pictures, weighed and measured, and *released it back to the water*. The mount of this twenty-two-pound northern pike ended up on the wall of her nail salon. Since she owned the place she could decorate it any way she wanted. You should have heard the reaction of some of those prim and proper, fastidious clients! And by the way, can you guess who paid for this mount? It never ends when you have a daughter.

"That's a keeper" is an important phrase on the tournament trail. When every ounce counts, that fish with a little extra weight makes the difference between feast and famine. I've seen a number of tournaments on TV where the best fish is caught in the last ten minutes. And what do those pros say? "Yes! Yes! Yes! That's a keeper!"

This phrase isn't limited to fishing. You and I are "keepers." In fact, every person ever created is a keeper in God's eyes. There's no culling that occurs on His part. No matter our size, shape, age, gender, color . . . it's all the same to Him. He says, "I want *you*." And why not? He created us. He took action so we could belong to Him forever.

"For God so loved the world that he gave his one and only Son, that whoever believes in him shall not perish but have eternal life" (John 3:16).

So it's all right to be a kept man or woman. There's a lot of security in that. The reason He sees us as a keeper is different than why we see a fish as a keeper. It's really simple. He loves us. Remember that. You're deeply loved and forever His. Why not tell another person, "I'm a keeper," and see where your conversation leads.

This is how God showed his love among us: He sent his one and only Son into the world that we might live through him.

—1 John 4:9

You Lost Your What?

2

The glasses broke the smooth surface of the lake and descended in a lazy arc to the sand six feet below. They landed with the lenses looking skyward as I stood there with my hand on the empty case in my shirt pocket. It was one of those moments that while it's happening you don't believe it's happening. And after you accept that it happened, you ask yourself two questions: "How in the world did I do that?" and "How am I going to retrieve them?"

It was a beautiful morning on Lake Arrowhead. I'd walked down a ramp to a dock and begun looking for some smallmouth I knew hung out there. That's when I leaned over for a closer look.

Well, I had to have those glasses, so I went all the way back along the shore, got into the car, drove to our cabin, and retrieved two "items." One was my wife, Joyce, and the other was a ten-foot collapsible pole to which I attached a small net. (When I told Joyce what happened, she responded, "You lost what?")

We walked back the half mile to the dock where we saw my glasses lying at the bottom of the lake just waiting to be fished out. My first effort with the pole and net did nothing to achieve the results I wanted. I buried them! Now all I could see was one stem poking out of the sand and Joyce looking at me wanting to say, "Would you like me to try?" but thinking that wouldn't be a good idea. I tried again and was successful ... in stirring up the sand and totally burying the glasses. By now I was disgusted, frustrated, and just knew those glasses were history. No one would find them now. I said that along with "Forget it. Let's just go, and I'll order some new ones." Fishing was a loss, because of the racket we were making. I walked back up the ramp, leaving Joyce standing there with the net attached to the pole and peering into the water.

I was gathering my fishing equipment as Joyce walked up the ramp with the pole extended in front of her. In the net were my glasses. She said she couldn't see them, prayed that the Lord would guide her hands, closed her eyes, and plunged the net into the sand and scooped ... and there they were!

How many times had that happened? I'd give up on something and Joyce would either find it or fix it. You'd think I'd learn. Those glasses were buried out of sight, and yet somehow she saw a way to find them. (Of course, she did ask for the Lord's help. Why didn't I think of that?) I guess it's true what they say about men having vision problems. We can be standing there looking for something and it's staring us right in the face, but we don't see it. Like opening the refrigerator and asking, "Yo, where's the mayo?" Our wife comes over and picks it right off the shelf in front of us. "This what you can't find, honey?" And then we mumble and grumble over our ineptness. How easy it is to just give up and say, "It's not there."

I'm glad I can count on one person never (and I mean *never*) giving up on me. God won't. God doesn't. He pursues us—He did this through His Son.

"For God did not send the Son into the world in order to judge—to reject, to condemn, to pass sentence on—the world; but that the world might find salvation and be made safe and sound through Him" (John 3:17 AMP). Safe and sound—doesn't that give you reassurance?

"All that the Father gives me will come to me, and whoever comes to me I will never drive away" (John 6:37). Never rejected by God! Can you imagine that?

"That is, in Christ, he chose us before the world was made so that we would be his holy people—people without blame before him. Because of his love, God had already decided to make us his own children through Jesus Christ. That was what he wanted and that pleased him" (Ephesians 1:4–5 NCV). I had pleasure in finding my glasses but *nothing* like God's pleasure in saving us.

My help comes from the Lord,
who made the heavens and the
earth! He will not let you stumble
and fall; the one who watches over
you will not sleep.... The Lord
himself watches over you!

—Psalm 121:2–3, 5 NLT

Smile—You're on Candid Camera

3

Imagine you're a four-pound bass swimming around some rocks with a buddy. You're eighteen feet deep. The water is dark and murky. All of a sudden there's a light attached to a small camera. You look at your buddy, and the conversation goes something like this:

"Would you look at this! Talk about an invasion of privacy. It's one thing to know there are sonar beams bouncing off us all the time from those fish locators."

"Wasn't it enough just knowing we're down here? Now they want to watch everything we do. What a bunch of voyeurs! Isn't anything sacred? Good grief."

"And look at the light on this gadget. Hey—let's see how much mud and silt we can stir up with our tails. Maybe that'll give us some privacy."

I wonder what bass do think about the controversial new cameras that have hit the scene. Perhaps you've made the investment so you can explore the depths and really discover what's down there.

How can this make a difference? Let's say your graph shows a bottom at thirty feet with no structure. It's a hard bottom, but that's about all there is. Or could there be more? Using the CatchCam you may discover a number of one- to two-foot boulders with several fish around them. Graphs sometimes eliminate boulders and even fish. I've noticed differences between the various fish locators I use.

A camera will show you pieces of structure that hold fish. And what appears as a rock on your graph may end up being a discarded battery or a chunk of concrete. Perhaps what you thought was grass on your graph turns out to be a school of baitfish.

What can a camera do? It's not just another adult toy (although they're a lot of fun to use). It can help you distinguish whether the fish you're graphing are large or small. It will help you understand your other electronics better. But . . . the purpose of this gadget is not to find fish and catch them. It helps you understand the environment of the fish better. It's another tool. But you still have to catch them.

Perhaps you haven't heard about this new camera. Take a look in the Bass Pro catalog at the Aqua-Vu. You can purchase one starting at $299 all the way up to $500. Some of our rods and reels cost that much. It will give you a third eye. To a bass, this eye from above is another threat. We sit in our boat, watching and observing.[1]

We're not much different than the bass. We're being watched.

We're being observed. We're being thought about. And it's a good thing.

This is a psalm I've memorized. I recite it several times a week. It reminds me who is watching me. It's reassuring. It's comforting. What would your life be like if you recited this several times a week?

> O Lord, you have examined my heart and know everything about me. You know when I sit or stand. When far away you know my every thought. You chart the path ahead of me and tell me where to stop and rest. Every moment, you know where I am. You know what I am going to say before I even say it. You both precede and follow me and place your hand of blessing on my head. . . . You made all the delicate, inner parts of my body and knit them together in my mother's womb. Thank you for making me so wonderfully complex! It is amazing to think about. Your workmanship is marvelous—and how well I know it. You were there while I was being formed in utter seclusion! You saw me before I was born and scheduled each day of my life before I began to breathe. Every day was recorded in your book! (Psalm 139:1–5, 13–16 TLB)

Whatever you do, do it all for the glory of God.

—1 Corinthians 10:1

Should I Imitate You?

$\mathcal{H}$ave you ever watched a child imitate his mom or dad? It happens all the time. That little child watches his parent like a hawk. He imitates the way his dad walks, talks, burps, frowns, flakes out on the couch, and even the way he fishes. It's true—even fishing falls under his scrutiny.

At Fork Lake in Texas I went out with an instructional guide. He was a wealth of information. He talked; I listened and learned. When I asked about his children, he told me about his daughter. She was bitten by the fishing bug real early in life. I thought my daughter was off to a running start when she hooked up, cast out, and landed her own barracuda at the age of six.

But this other little girl beat that. When Daddy came home from a fishing tournament, she stood in the doorway and informed him she wanted to fish in a tournament! I guess her confidence level was intact.

My guide told me that from time to time he's asked by different groups to give classes. One group requested a class on flippin'—nothing else, just flippin'. He decided to spend some time practicing and perfecting his skill. So he went out in the backyard and practiced several casts. His little girl, who was just three at the time, came out and wanted to learn. Not only did he patiently take the time to teach her, but he had a pro rod cut down to fit her size. If he practiced a hundred casts, she made a hundred. If he did two hundred, so did she. And as he improved, so did she. That takes a lot of work, because a three-year-old's muscle strength and coordination haven't developed much.

The day he went to the class, he decided to take her along. As he began to show the group how to flip, some of them just sat there and shook their heads. One Texan voiced the sentiments of a number of them: "You make it look so easy. You've probably done this thousands of times. I don't think I'll ever get the hang of it."

The guide's response was, "Don't give up. You can get it. Just watch. I'm going to show my three-year-old daughter how to flip. And if she can do it, so can you." His daughter came up. He gave her some basic instruction, and she started flippin' that plastic grub out there just like her daddy. When the men saw the ease with which she did it, they got a boost in their confidence, got with the program, and learned to flip.

Let's face it: whether we want to be or not, we're models. People are going to watch us, learn from us, and in some way represent us when we're not around. We're being watched whether we realize it or not.

When we're out on the lake fishing, what *would* others learn if they were watching us? I don't mean when we're catching one fish after another and every cast is falling two inches from where we intended. What would they learn when we bend our trolling motor on a log or we get a glorious backlash in our Calcutta 2000, or we miss the lip of that nine-pound bass at the edge of the boat and watch it disappear into the depths. That's when our real character is seen.

I've heard some say, "I really don't care what others think about me." That's all right if you don't know Jesus. But if you do, you're representing Him. We're not to live for ourselves but for Him. Paul said it like this:

> For Christ's love compels us, because we are convinced that one died for all, and therefore all died. And he died for all, that those who live should no longer live for themselves but for him who died for them and was raised again. (2 Corinthians 5:14–15)
>
> Whatever you have learned or received or heard from me, or seen in me—put it into practice. And the God of peace will be with you. (Philippians 4:9)

If others modeled their lives after what they see in us, would we want to be around them? It's something to think about.

It is a badge of honor to accept valid criticism.

—Proverbs 25:12 TLB

Me? Defensive? Never

5

$\mathscr{A}$ friend and I were at one of the largest fishing and boating shows in California. As we strolled the aisles we noticed one of the exhibits for salmon fishing in Alaska. It was like many others, except the guides manning the booth were all women. As we talked with them, I asked if many women went on their excursions. They told us quite a few did, then added a comment I didn't expect: "And they always catch more fish than the men."

I asked, "Why is that?"

"It's simple. The women listen to what we tell them to do. They're more open to instruction than the men." Interesting. That's quite a commentary on us men. That is, if that's *really* true! (How's that for a typical male response?) But I've heard the same comment from other guides, including men. A couple of bass guides complained to me about the very same thing. One said, "I wonder why some clients bother to hire me for a day. They end up telling *me* how they're going to catch fish with their dumb lures. It usually takes a couple of hours for them to listen."

What is it about males that makes us resistant to instruction and advice? We seem to have this need to show how much we know about something. If I'm out with a guide who's been bass fishing for years, I want every bit of knowledge he's got.

Fishing isn't the only place we men aren't that open to instruction. We often react the same way in our marriage relationships (yeah, yeah, I know I'm meddling now).

I remember reading the following about men (and I remember *my* reaction). Here's the gist of what was said:

Men hate to be wrong. (I'm not sure I agree with this.)

They hate being told they're wrong. (True.)

They hate even to suspect that they might have been wrong. (Whoa! That's going a bit too far.)

And most of all, men hate it when a woman knows that they are wrong before they know it themselves. (*Very* true.)

The tricky part is, men feel they are being "made wrong" or told they did something wrong, when you aren't telling them that at all. (Guilty as charged.)

Those statements give you a lot to think about, don't they?

I found an interesting study about marriages that last compared to those that don't. After all was said and done it came down to one principle: "Newlywed men who listened to what their wives said and did it ended up with stable marriages."[2]

There's another source for telling us to listen to advice. It's God's Word. Consider these words the next time you're tempted to tune out that person giving you advice:

Be not wise in your own eyes. (Proverbs 3:7 AMP)

A man who refuses to admit his mistakes can never be successful. But if he confesses and forsakes them, he gets another chance. (Proverbs 28:13 TLB)

He who leans on, trusts in and is confident of his own mind and heart is a [self-confident] fool, but he who walks with skillful and godly Wisdom shall be delivered. (Proverbs 28:26 AMP)

If you want some real advice that can change your life, read the book of Proverbs, then apply it. Your work relationships, your family relationships, *and* your fishing relationships—they'll all see the difference.

And the peace of God, which
transcends all understanding, will
guard your hearts and your minds
in Christ Jesus.

—Philippians 4:7

Peace—It's Possible

6

$\mathcal{A}$ gag rule—that's what my fishing partner and I sometimes employ when we go out to the lake. We put a lid on certain subjects so we don't talk about them while we're fishing. Pursuing bass is a time to do just that—not bring the daily hassles along with us. Being a counselor working with people in grief and trauma, I don't want to have those issues follow me into the boat. It's easy, especially for men, to leave their work behind physically but not mentally. On the lake, though, we need peace.

There are two items we need to leave at home when we fish: the radio and the cell phone. Water acts as an amplifier, and who wants to listen to the beat of what some call music or the fluctuations of the stock market? I don't know how many conversations I've had to hear from another angler a hundred feet away as he talks to his office on his cell phone.

One morning I met my partner at a lake to fish from shore. I wish I'd gotten there ten minutes earlier. It had rained the day before so the bank was *very* slick. He had his beeper on his belt along with his cell phone. His first step on the slope down to the edge was the only one he had to take. He just kept on going, and at the edge of the bank he launched—right into four feet of water. You know, electronics don't work too well when they're submerged.

Life goes on—the world goes on when we're out of touch. Perhaps we think we're indispensable. We're not.

Some have said, "I've got to stay in touch. They might need me." Or, "I'll miss that business deal." "Hey, it's a cutthroat world out there. You've got to be on your guard. It's not that safe. So I have to stay in touch." We think we're in control. We think we're in charge of everything. We can't relax. We have to worry and we miss the joy of life and the peace God's offered to us. Leave the stuff home, and really, I mean *really*, go fishing. And whether you're at home, at work, or fishing, begin to experience what the presence of Jesus can do in your life.

In the gospel of Matthew we read that Jesus and His disciples were in a boat once when "without warning, a furious storm came up on the lake." This was a common occurrence on the Sea of Galilee. The disciples were frantic, but the next text says Jesus was taking a nap (Matthew 8:24–27).

Here is what one of my favorite authors, John Ortberg, says about this story and what you and I can experience:

> Given what he knew about the Father, Jesus was convinced that the universe was a perfectly safe place for him to be.

The disciples had faith in Jesus. They trusted that he could do something to help them. They did not share his settled conviction that they were safe in God's hands.

This is what Paul called "the peace of Christ."[3]

Perhaps we all need to consider what our lives would look like if we lived in the conviction of who God is and the power of His presence. John Ortberg describes the results:

- My anxiety level would go down. I would have the settled trust that my life is perfectly at rest in the hands of God. I would not be tormented by my own inadequacy.
- I would be an unhurried person. I might be busy, might have many things to do, but I would have an inner calmness and poise that comes from being in the presence of God. I would not say so many of the foolish things I now say because I speak without thinking.
- I would not be defeated by guilt. I would live in the confidence that comes from the assurance of God's love.
- I would trust God enough to risk obeying him. I wouldn't have to hoard. Worry makes me focus on myself. It robs me of joy, energy, and compassion.
- A person in whom the peace of Christ reigns would be an oasis of sanity in a world of pandemonium.
- A community in which the peace of Christ reigns would change the world.[4]

*As iron sharpens iron, so one
man sharpens another.*

—Proverbs 27:17

The Loner

7

You're fifteen feet under the surface of the lake. Above, the sun is shining, the trees on the shore are various shades of green and brown, and the sky seems endless. It's a different story where you are. It's murky, and what vegetation there is seems drab and even lifeless. A crawdad skirts from the protection of one rock to the other, and a couple of shad slip by. There are two or three large boulders and an aged tree stump, and that's all. But hold it. There is something else.

There's a large solitary shape between the tree and one of the rocks. You look closer. It's a bass, a *large* bass with a torn fin and a few scars on its body. There are no other fish around. And that's the way she wants it. She's solitary and in a world of her own. When she sees a school of shad she doesn't alert any other bass so they can share in the feast. Nor does she work together with three or four others to ambush and harvest the shad. Her motto is "I'd rather do it myself," and she does. No hassles with other bass. No responsibility. No accountability. She just lives life by herself, for herself, with no interaction with other fish.

We were created for relationships. And relationships include accountability. We're not to be an island unto ourselves or a solitary "trophy bass." And even when you see a school of bass, they're hanging out together but they're really *not* together. They have no interaction, no accountability, and no fellowship.

Relationships are one of the most significant elements of life. We were created to be in relationships, not to exist without them. Most of our lives are spent in various relationships. Take them away, and our existence becomes sterile. Sure, there are those who appear not to need them, but they're the exceptions.

Max Lucado has something to say about relationships:

> A relationship. The delicate fusion of two human beings. The intricate weaving of two lives; two sets of moods, mentalities, and temperaments. Two intermingling hearts, both seeking solace and security.
>
> A relationship. It has more power than any nuclear bomb and more potential than any promising seed. Nothing will drive a man to greater courage than a relationship. Nothing will fire the heart of a patriot or purge the cynicism of a rebel like a relationship.
>
> What matters most in life is not what ladders we climb or what ownings we accumulate. What matters most is a relationship.[5]

How would you describe your relationships with others? How would they describe them?

And then there's accountability. To whom are you accountable? Who is accountable to you?

Why be accountable? Patrick Morley describes it for us:

> The purpose of accountability is nothing less than to each day become more Christ-like in all our ways and ever more intimate with Him.
>
> Unless we are answerable on a regular basis for the key areas of our personal lives we, like sheep, will go astray. Yet, to submit our lives for inspection to someone else grates on our desire to be independent. While we desire to live like a Christian, we often want to keep it just between "me and Jesus." But the way of the Scriptures points to accountability among believers.[6]

> Brothers, if someone is caught in a sin, you who are spiritual should restore him gently. But watch yourself, or you also may be tempted. Carry each other's burdens, and in this way you will fulfill the law of Christ. (Galatians 6:1–2)
>
> Each of you should look not only to your own interests, but also to the interests of others. (Philippians 2:4)
>
> A new command I give to you: Love one another. As I have loved you, so you must love one another. (John 13:34)
>
> Two are better than one, because they have a good return for their work: If one falls down, his friend can help him up. But pity the man who falls and has no one to help him up! (Ecclesiastes 4:9–10)
>
> Faithful are the wounds of a friend; profuse are the kisses of an enemy. (Proverbs 27:6 RSV)

In what way is each of these passages reflected in your life?

It is better not to vow than to make a vow and not fulfill it.

—Ecclesiastes 5:5

I'll Take You Fishing ... Someday

"I'll take you fishing ... someday." How many kids have heard that statement from a well-meaning adult? For some, someday never comes. It's a dream that fades a little with each passing year.

Who took you fishing for the first time? Do you remember that experience? What you remember may not be what you caught but the experience itself.

I grew up in the hills of Hollywood. There was no water around. But my parents made sure I fished. If one couldn't take me, the other did. And if they said we were going fishing, we went. They kept their word. I have many memories—fishing off the pier, the deep-sea boats, and the barge—and there we always caught fish.

We went to lakes, the Colorado River, lagoons, and small ponds. We didn't always catch fish. That was okay. We went fishing.

When you take someone fishing, you've got to have patience. He's probably not at your level. There is nothing better than seeing that child (or adult) pull in the first fish he's ever caught. And often he's there because you kept your word.

At one of the lakes I fish, the management invited the residents of a group home for troubled children to come and fish for the day. The kids were ecstatic. They looked forward to this day for weeks. When they arrived, the staff gave them lunch, then outfitted each one with a rod and reel and turned them loose on the dock and shore to fish. But no one stayed around to teach them. I'd finished fishing for bass, and when I got to the dock there were fifteen to twenty kids fishing from it. No one had caught a fish. I could see why. Each pole had a bobber and about three inches of line with a single hook hanging below.

We just happened to have some old tubs of catfish stink bait and treble spring hooks in the van. In a few minutes, the outfits were changed. The rancid bait hit the water. The next two hours were full of excitement and laughter as the kids started pulling in six- to nine-pound catfish off the dock. They weren't too keen about putting the stink bait on the hooks, so I had a steady stream of kids asking me to put it on. Those were the best two hours I spent that day. Those kids were making some happy memories.

Sure, they didn't know what they were doing. Sure, they made mistakes and got in the way. They were a lot like you and me.

Who do you know that wants to go fishing with you?

Who do you know that needs to go fishing with you?

If you offer, follow through; keep your word. If you don't, you lose your credibility. Promises are made to be kept not only in this area of life but in every area.

If you tell someone you'll pray for him, pray.

If you tell someone you'll be there, then be there.

If you promise to love a person and be faithful for life, do that. The Word of God has something to say about keeping our word.

> Therefore each of you must put off falsehood and speak truthfully to his neighbor, for we are all members of one body. (Ephesians 4:25)
>
> And whatever you do, whether in word or deed, do it all in the name of the Lord Jesus, giving thanks to God the Father through him. (Colossians 3:17)
>
> Lord, who may dwell in your sanctuary? Who may live on your holy hill? He whose walk is blameless and who does what is righteous, who speaks the truth from his heart. (Psalm 15:1–2)
>
> When a man makes a vow to the Lord or takes an oath to obligate himself by a pledge, he must not break his word but must do everything he said. (Numbers 30:2)

Jesus made a promise to you. He promised He would return someday. He'll keep His Word. He wants us to keep ours.

*You can't live your Christian life
without a connection—prayer.*

Stick That Fish

9

"Stick it to him."

"Set it as hard as you can and then some."

If you've been around bass anglers, you've heard these phrases yelled from one angler to another when a bass hits. You've also probably heard fishing involves "a jerk on one end of a pole waiting for a jerk on the other end."

How do you set the hook when your fish hits? Do you give a super fast flick of the wrist that's so slight it's hard to see? Some do. Or do you use the stoutest rod possible, tighten the reel's drag down as far as it will go, and haul back so hard that occasionally you break the rod? Some do.

Techniques and methods vary, but hook setting is a critical part of fishing. How would you describe what you do? And is there any variation depending on the equipment you're using? Perhaps you've never given it much thought. You need to. I've seen too many fish lost (including my own) because of an improperly set hook.

Have you heard of the "regular set"? Most use this when they're using soft plastics, some types of pork rinds, and live baits. When you feel that familiar tap, you lean forward, extend your arms and rod tip toward the fish, at the same time reeling in the slack line this creates, and then striking back with the rod and your hands high over your head.

Then there's the speed set. This is used with crankbaits, spinnerbaits, or other lures. The line is usually already tight when you set the hook. Your fish sets the hook in this situation as much as you do. Your offering is moving along at a good rate of speed and it doesn't yield, since your line is already tight. So the hooks penetrate. Any action you take is more for insurance.

You've probably engaged in the interchange of "got him," and then "missed him" with another angler. When might this problem occur more often—with the regular set or the speed set? Research indicates the speed set is more effective.

Have you used the two-handed set? It's twice as effective as a one-handed set, whether you're using spinning or bait casting rods. It's a very quick maneuver. The instant you feel a strike you take your hand from the reel handle and place it high up on the rod above the reel. Then with a hard jerk pull back with the high hand and push down with the low hand. When your fish is hooked, put your hand back on the handle and crank.

When you really haul back, make sure you have solid footing and a stable boat. Otherwise, you'll join the fish. A couple of instructional guides have drilled into me the principle of properly setting the hook. I'm grateful for their expertise as well as reminders. It's easy to become lazy. Keep this formula in mind: What's your ratio of setting the hook to actual fish hooked? That may give you insight into the effectiveness of your methods.

All of the above is immaterial if one other factor isn't present. You can have the smoothest, fastest, most creative setting technique, but if your hook isn't super sharp, forget it. You've got to have a hook that can penetrate every area of a bass's mouth. Some areas are hard gristle, and your hook may just slide over it and not dig in. Use quality hooks. Change hooks frequently. Sharpen your hooks. And keep them sharp.[7]

So regardless of your hook-setting technique, it really boils down to this one element: how sharp is your hook?

It's sort of like that in our Christian walk. There are people who talk like Christians, involve themselves in as many church activities as they can, read devotional books as well as the Bible, but something is lacking in their life. There's no spiritual depth or power. They've got the language and the involvement, but they are missing what changes lives—prayer.

You can't live your Christian life without a connection—prayer. Scripture tells us, "Devote yourselves to prayer" (Colossians 4:2). How often do you pray? What is it like when you pray? Does it feel like a rote routine or more like you've really talked with someone? When do you pray? Simple questions, but the answers may tell you a lot about your life.

Have you thought about prayer being a privilege? Well, it is. Just think for a moment who you're conversing with. God himself.

And He wants to listen to you. What does that say about how special *you are?* If you want your life to really count for the kingdom of God, don't try to go it alone.

Jesus said, "I am the vine; you are the branches . . . apart from me you can do nothing" (John 15:5).

He is the power source for *your* life.

Nature Calls

10

$\mathcal{E}$ven if you've watched scores of bass tournaments on TV, I know there's one thing you've never seen. What happens when nature calls and there are boats all around or TV cameras trying to record every cast and strike? What's worse is when something you ate is doing the tango in your lower intestine, frantically looking for the quickest way out.

Have you been there yet? If not, just wait. It hits all of us . . . I know!

My wife, Joyce, and I were fishing in the late afternoon off the shore and docks at a mountain lake. All of a sudden my lunch told me it wanted out and in a hurry. I walked as fast as I could to the rest room about fifty yards away. The closer I got the faster I walked. I reached for the door and said, "No! They didn't! Those clowns!" There was a padlock on it and no way to break in. I looked around back and saw some bushes that would shield me from the shoreline and the homes on the hillside. A few minutes later I walked back to the lake, and Joyce said, "Hey, you were gone quite a while. You okay?"

I responded, "Oh yeah. No problem." (I was still questioning the sanity of those responsible for the locked bathroom!)

We decided to leave when it got dark, so with our equipment and Sheffield, our dog, in tow, we walked back to the tree-filled ravine that had 130 steps to climb to get to our car. About a third of the way up I began to experience a familiar rumbling sensation in the inner recesses of my body. I knew what it meant. It was the feeling of an inner avalanche. I'd never make it to the top, let alone to the house. I told Joyce, "I'm not going to make it. Wait here. I'm going back to the rest room."

I started down the steps and heard, "Don't leave me here without the flashlight. There are critters in those trees, and leave Sheffield too." I was in no position to argue so I tossed her the flashlight and leash and began taking two steps at a time . . . in the dark. (Real smart!) During my sprint it dawned on me. *It's a locked bathroom and I used my handkerchief the last time.* Being a man of keen insight, resourcefulness, and practicality (I don't think Joyce and my friends describe it that way), I pulled my shirt out of the front of my pants, then my eight-inch buck knife from my pocket, and as I leapt down the stairs in the dark I hacked off the shirttails.

I returned a few minutes later, and Joyce asked, "Well, what happened?"

All I said very casually was, "No problem. Let's go home."

Everything was fine until we walked into the cabin and she saw the front of my shirt minus the shirttails. In fact, the front was about an inch above my waistline. So I told her what had happened. All she said was, "Had you thought about cutting off the shirttails in the back? It might have looked better," but her rolling eyes sure said a lot.

Hey, in my condition and under those circumstances, thinking logically wasn't an option.

This was just one of numerous experiences over the years. Was I the only one to create memories like this? Get a group of anglers together to swap stories, and you'll end up laughing.

Only recently has this problem been addressed in bass fishing magazines. In *Bass West*, I found an ad for RESTOP, a disposable travel toilet with a clever Web site: *When Nature Calls.* In the same issue, Carol Martens had an article on this subject entitled "SOS Relief."

She said this problem is a number one concern, especially if both genders are in the same boat. Some lakes have bathrooms around the shoreline or even floating bathrooms. If not, in a boat you learn to turn your back or put a poncho around you. Carol told the story of a friend of hers pre-fishing a tournament at Lake Mead. The fellow told his female companion that he needed to go to the bathroom, so he beached the boat and disappeared out of sight over a hill. But a minute later he reappeared at the top of the hill, yelling, "Get the boat started!" He proceeded to hobble down the hill with his pants around his ankles and the biggest beaver you've ever seen snapping at his rear end. And it never let up. It hissed and snapped at his buns all the way to the boat. Can you picture it? That ol' beaver was probably having thoughts like, *Don't use my backyard for your bathroom!* or *It's revenge time for making my ancestors into top hats.*[8]

The moral of this story is—be careful. Before you do what needs to be done, look around.

And one other suggestion—God created you with the need to go to the bathroom. Ever thought of that? Nature calls are a part of life. Many experiences are going to be funny. So learn to laugh a little. Better yet, laugh a lot. After all, it's biblical.

Ecclesiastes 3:1, 4, states, "There is ... a time to laugh," and this is one of those times. A healthy sense of humor about our humanity and frailties keeps a balance in our life. It's especially helpful if we can laugh at ourselves. Sure, some experiences may be a bit embarrassing. But you know what? Others understand. We've all been there ... and that's reassuring.

A cheerful heart is good medicine.

—*Proverbs 17:22*

Lessons From a Light Eater

11

$\mathcal{L}$et's get personal. If I accompanied you to a buffet, what would I see? Would you be selective or would you take as much as you could eat and then some? People vary. I've seen some take a one-week cruise to the Caribbean and not gain a pound. I also heard of a man who gained twenty-four pounds in a week! Figure out how many calories that must have been. Some eat out of hunger, but some for other reasons.

What about a bass? Why does he strike a lure? It could be protecting a nest, reflex, or anger, but probably 95 percent of the time it's hunger. You've seen a school of bass on a feeding frenzy ripping through a school of shad. How many are really consumed? How many shad would a bass eat in a day? One, five, fifteen? You may be in for a surprise.

Let's look at Billy Bass. (No, I don't mean the singing rubber mount!) He's a two-pounder swimming around in an Oklahoma lake with a good supply of Threadfin shad. How often will he eat and how much? Biologists tell us a bass needs to eat three percent of its body weight each day if it's to grow in a normal manner, but only needs one percent to maintain its present weight as well as stay healthy. That works out to an ounce of shad every twenty-four hours for growth. And since the average shad is three to four inches long and weighs one-and-a-half ounces, Billy Bass needs to eat one shad every day and a half. That's not very many.

In another study, over nine hundred bass were monitored from spring through fall, with water temperatures varying from sixty-eight to eighty-two degrees. When tested, roughly half had empty stomachs. Of those that had food in their stomachs, 90 percent of the time just one item—usually a shad—was found. But what if a bass tried to gorge itself? Biologists have found the most a bass can eat and digest in twenty-four hours is twelve percent of its body weight.

When *does* he eat? Usually April through October is his best time. November through March is Weight Watchers time. He needs one shad a week to maintain his weight, but sometimes doesn't eat even that and loses some weight.

So according to this study, Billy Bass eats about eighty-four shad a year to grow. (I think I've met a number of bass that are exceptions to this.) He may not be the feeding fish you thought he was. Sure, if he's four or six or ten pounds he'll eat more. But probably not what you thought. He does have limits.[9]

Let's get to meddling. How are your feeding habits?

Some eat to live and others live to eat. I've seen a lot of anglers who are in great shape and really take care of their bodies. They eat right and exercise regularly. (Sorry, casting does not qualify as an aerobic exercise.) But I've seen others who have a hard time standing up in their boat without putting it off balance. Their body is off balance. There's more food on some boats than tackle.

I've heard people say, "What I eat is my business. My body is my business." Well, the truth is, it's not. We belong to Christ, which means so does our body. The Scripture says, "Do you not know that your body is the temple—the very sanctuary—of the Holy Spirit Who lives within you, Whom you have received [as a Gift] from God? You are not your own" (1 Corinthians 6:19 AMP).

Proverbs 23:21 states, "The glutton shall come to poverty" (AMP).

Unfortunately, some bodies resemble a rotunda more than a temple of the Holy Spirit. What we put into our body does matter. Keeping our body in shape does matter. If we can discipline ourselves to be proficient in catching bass, what about discipline in other areas? How we choose to treat our body could reflect on our relationship with Jesus.

The next time you're tempted at the buffet, remember Billy Bass. He may have had one shad today. And then again, maybe not.

So then, just as you received Christ Jesus as Lord, continue to live in him, rooted and built up in him, strengthened in the faith as you were taught.

—Colossians 2:6–7

A "Reel" Angler

12

We've all met them. You can't miss them. They stick out and make themselves known. They're the wanna-be bass anglers and pros.

These anglers have the trappings of someone who's into catching bass. They seem to have it all—the boat, the rods and reels, even the high-tech electronics including the Aqua-Vu. Their tackle cases would rival a bass pro shop in selection from sizes to colors. They're "reel" bass anglers. Just ask them. On second thought, don't ask them. You don't need to. They'll tell you what they can do and what they've got. They seem to have it all with the exception of one item—fish. They're lacking what it's all about. I've even seen some chuck everything after a while. It wasn't what they really wanted.

The wanna-be pro can border on the obnoxious. I had to deal

with one for months, since he was the manager of a lake I fished. He was quick to let you know this was just a temporary job. He was honing his skills so he could hit the circuit. His experience in tournaments was minimal and his results were even less. It was interesting to watch. He'd let others know about his abilities and his dreams on the one hand, but on the other grill them to learn how they were catching fish that day. It didn't matter if the angler had only been fishing for six months or this was his first day, he'd get the third degree. And the response was as if the "pro" had never heard the information before, even if it was Bass Basics 101. This guy wanted to be someone, be around those who were known as pros, but he wasn't one himself. And it was doubtful that he would ever be the real article.

Some Christians are like this. They're not really "reel."

Jesus talked about this in the parable of the sower:

"Those along the path are the ones who hear, and then the devil comes and takes away the word from their hearts, so that they may not believe and be saved" (Luke 8:12).

Some hear about Jesus but reject him.

"Those on the rock are the ones who receive the word with joy when they hear it, but they have no root. They believe for a while, but in the time of testing they fall away" (Luke 8:13).

Some try being Christians, but then turn their backs on it. There's another type as well:

"The seed that fell among thorns stands for those who hear,

but as they go on their way they are choked by life's worries, riches and pleasures, and they do not mature" (Luke 8:14).

This is the Christian that you don't always know is a believer. He wants the best of both worlds. He says he's a Christian, just like some people call themselves "anglers," but neither really produces.

We're called to be like the following person:

"But the seed on good soil stands for those with a noble and good heart, who hear the word, retain it, and by persevering produce a crop" (Luke 8:15).

We're called to be "reel": genuine, trusting in Christ, and growing in such a way that our life reflects our faith. This involves learning the teachings of Jesus, applying them, being willing to be different, and allowing the Holy Spirit to give us the power to do just that.

So here's your question: When others see you on the lake, do they say, "He's a true angler"?

And when others see you living your life, do they say, "He's definitely a Christian. His life shows it"?

𝒟on't be anxious about tomorrow. God will take care of your tomorrow too. Live one day at a time.

—Matthew 6:34 TLB

Too Busy

13

"Hey, I'm too busy to go fishing." Not too many true anglers make that statement. But this disease is always lurking just around the corner waiting to infect our lives, and when it does, say good-bye to the presence of joy. They're not compatible.

It used to be when people asked "How are you doing?" we'd say "Fine." Now we too often reply, "Busy."

I've been on lakes where the scenery and wildlife are like a *National Geographic* documentary. Even if the fishing wasn't good, the surroundings made up for it. I've made comments to other anglers about rugged cliffs, the vegetation, or various animals. Sometimes I hear the response, "I didn't notice. I'm too busy trying to find some bass."

Well, it's true that men are single-minded and incredibly focused, but all it takes is a minute to stop, look around, and listen.

Sometimes the sounds call you back to what you're missing. It could be the gentle breeze rustling the leaves of the trees, the cry of a hawk, the call of a loon, or the splash of a beaver. Look up; look around. What you see may be better than catching a large bass.

I was shore fishing on a small mountain lake and looked up. Two bald eagles were fighting with a golden eagle over a fish one of them had caught. They tumbled through the air again and again. I stopped fishing to watch a sight I'd never seen before and perhaps never would again.

Busyness can keep us from getting the most out of life. Even bass pros battle this problem.

Some men say they wish they could have the life of a pro—all the pros have to do is fish and get paid for it. They've never talked to a pro about his life. One told me he was away from his home for four months straight. He'd finish a tournament, go to a show to promote a boat or rod for one of his sponsors, drive to another lake to pre-fish for three days, fish the tournament, and then drive to the next one. In the meantime, he had to keep up his boat, change line, replace lost items, keep in contact with family. . . . You get the picture. Some may thrive on this. Others get worn out. This guide said his lifestyle cost him his marriage. He was too busy.

It's too bad life gets so busy. Busyness impacts our life in many ways. It can cloud our judgment and discernment. When we have too much to do we don't take the time to think about decisions. Mahatma Gandhi said, "There is more to life than increasing its speed." Someone else said, "Nothing done impulsively and in a hurry is ever well done. . . . We always do fast enough when we do well. Drones make more noise and are more in a hurry than the

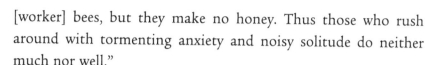

[worker] bees, but they make no honey. Thus those who rush around with tormenting anxiety and noisy solitude do neither much nor well."

Often busyness is connected to accumulation—that could be reputation as well as money.

Jesus said, "For whoever wants to save his life will lose it, but whoever loses his life for me will find it. What good will it be for a man if he gains the whole world, yet forfeits his soul? Or what can a man give in exchange for his soul?" (Matthew 16:25–26).

Does God call us to a life of busyness? No. He calls us to a life of balance. There's a little word that can help to put a lid on busyness: *No.* Say it to others and to yourself.

*The wise man is glad to be
instructed.*

—Proverbs 10:8 TLB

A Bass Isn't the Only Thing That Bites

It's the ultimate in bass lures. If you don't have this revolutionary lure, that's why you're not catching fish. It rattles. It shakes. It shimmers. It glows. It's even got a flashing light powered by a hearing-aid battery. Guaranteed to catch fish." You sit there glued to the TV, watching bass after bass fall to this new lure. (Could it be the same fish from twenty different angles?) Your hand begins to twitch. You reach for your pen to write down that 800 number, grab your credit card, and head for the phone. You're hooked!

The TV and magazine ads look so inviting with their promises of fishing you've never experienced before. I've seen a number of these describing the newest and ultimate lure. I'll admit it. I've bitten a few times. I remember one (I won't mention the name, although it was similar to a guitar). The lure looked great, but you had to screw in a wire so you could tie it to the line. It seemed to have a built-in obsolescence—use it once and it's history! I went back to my main line lures and caught bass again.

I guess we're all looking for something new, something better, something guaranteed. But hard work, practice, and learning from others works better. It's easy to fall for the advertising, to respond on impulse without taking time to think.

What about you?

Do *you* believe everything you hear? I mean, how do *you* respond to some of those TV commercials or infomercials about lures?

The book of Proverbs has some advice to remember:

"A simple man believes anything, but a prudent man gives thought to his steps" (Proverbs 14:15). This verse provides a warning that may help us stay out of difficulty. In another version, it says, "The naïve believes everything, but the prudent man considers his steps" (NASB).

The Hebrew word for *simple* or *naïve* presents the idea of open-mindedness or inexperience that leaves a person open to being conned. One writer describes the naïve as "a person of undecided views and thus susceptible to either good or bad influences."[10] Do you know anyone like this?

Simple people are way too trusting. They're gullible and believe just about anything. They lack a discerning spirit. The Bible says they like the way they are. Proverbs asks the question, "How long, O simple ones and open [to evil], will you love being simple?" (1:22 AMP). Perhaps the reason is they rarely consider the consequences of what they do. They enjoy being open-minded. They also lack good moral sense. They're lousy judges of character, and they often develop friendships with others like themselves. They can't seem to recognize evil. "A prudent man sees the evil and hides himself, but the simple pass on and are punished (with suffering)" (Proverbs 22:3 AMP).

Is there hope for this person? How will he or she turn out?

If we're naïve, it comes back to haunt us. Proverbs 14:18 says, "The simple inherit folly, but the prudent are crowned with knowledge."

One of the best ways to overcome being naïve is found in the Word of God.

> The law of the Lord is perfect, restoring the soul; the testimony of the Lord is sure, making wise the simple [naïve]. (Psalm 19:7 NASB, bracketed word is author's)
>
> The unfolding of Thy words gives light; it gives understanding to the simple [naïve]. (Psalm 119:130 NASB, bracketed word is author's)

So the next time you read or watch that promising ad, slow down, think, and consider what these slick ads are all about. One thing is obvious—they're geared to hook you into buying. And when you're enticed by other temptations in life, don't bite. Go back to the Word of God—that's your strength.

Hold on to instruction, do not let it go; guard it well, for it is your life.

—Proverbs 4:13

The Two Guys From...

15

$\mathcal{G}$uides are a rich source for wild and zany fishing experiences. I've heard some crazy ones that I can pass on as well as some that can't be put in print. A guide in Texas told me about two guys he hopes he never hears from again. They called from Michigan and set up two days of fishing on Fork Lake. They wanted to fish this lake in the worst way. Now, since they were coming from Michigan, you'd think they would have checked the weather ahead of time or at least would have brought some warm clothes. They didn't.

The day they arrived at the dock it was fourteen degrees. And the temperature was expected to rise only about twenty degrees! Not only that, the wind was already up to fifteen miles per hour with predictions of moving up to thirty-five miles per hour later in the day. Not a pleasant outlook. The guide asked them if they really wanted to go out on the lake. Their response: "Why not?"

He explained, but they said, "Well, so . . . we're from Michigan. We can handle it."

So they went out. It was cold . . . and windy . . . and . . . wet. The guide wasn't very hopeful. The water was bad. The weather was worse. If they got one or two strikes that day, let alone fish, they'd be lucky! He could tell these guys didn't know a whole lot and weren't the best students. They battled the storm and got to a somewhat secluded spot. One fished the stern and the other one, a very large man, took the middle. The guy at the back got a bite from a huge bass and broke it off. That could have been the only fish of the day.

They'd both been shown how to haul back on the rod and really set the hook. The guy in the middle got a bite and followed the instructions to the letter—only instead of rearing back with the rod to his right or his left, he came straight back, as hard as he could with all his weight into it, and hit himself right between the eyes. He stood there, stunned, dropped the rod and lost his fish. His friend and the guide looked at him, mouths open. The wind's blowing, the boat's rocking, and this guy is just standing there in a daze, his glasses barely on his face. One lens covers one eye and one lens covers the other, but the nose bridge is shattered. A welt is forming on his forehead. And he stands there saying, "I missed him. I dropped the pole," over and over again. And all this happened during the first hour! Somehow the guide knew this was going to be a long, long day.

He noticed the other guy's lips were blue and he was shivering. "What are you wearing?" the guide asked him.

The fellow's teeth chattered as he said, "Just this sweat suit with shorts underneath. I thought Texas would be warmer!" The guide ran the boat to shore and sent them off to Wal-Mart to buy some warm clothes. They came back with insulated jackets.

The wind had picked up, so they found a sheltered location. Once again the guide reminded them, "Remember, when a bass hits, haul back and set that hook!" They each got a strike and each missed it. The guide had his back turned but felt the boat lurch, heard a splash, turned around to see the guy at the back of the boat had disappeared—vanished. Just then he broke the surface, spitting water and still holding his rod. He proceeded to hold it up and pirouetted like a ballet dancer, then promptly sank again. When he popped up for air, his buddy, the large guy, leaned over the boat and hoisted him out of the lake and onto the deck. Needless to say, the guy was soaked and near frozen.

They raced to shore and the guide told them where his house was—gave them the keys, told them to get out of the wet clothes and into a warm shower, and then to bundle up in blankets. But after the guide had taken his boat out of the water and arrived at his house, he found the two men sitting in front of the house in their truck—the motor off—wet and miserable. They had decided to stay in their truck, keep the engine running, with the heat on high—but they ran out of gas.

Before you think this was an extraordinarily wild day for these two would-be fishermen, there's more. As the guide helped them recover, he found out that this day's adventure was typical. They'd had similar ones back in Michigan. Like getting rescued off ice floes that had broken off as they fished, being rescued by a helicopter, and several other misadventures.

The guide made a wise decision. His parting comment was "Ya' know, the weather prediction for tomorrow is the same as today, and something has come up and I'm not available tomorrow. Wish I could help you out, but here's the card of a buddy of mine. Y'all give him a call, okay?" And that's the last he saw of them.

You wonder if guys like this learn anything from their experiences. As we go through life we're supposed to change, grow, and profit from what happens to us. That's what it tells us in Scripture.

For acquiring a disciplined and prudent life, doing what is right and just and fair . . . the fear of the Lord is the beginning of knowledge, but fools despise wisdom and discipline. (Proverbs 1:3, 7)

Hear counsel, receive instruction and accept correction, that you may be wise in the time to come. (Proverbs 19:20 AMP)

Listen to my instruction and be wise; do not ignore it. (Proverbs 8:33)

Can you think of ways you've learned from your experiences?

Are you open to instruction? If not, your life will probably run into misadventures like those of the two anglers from Michigan. Instead, I hope you'll reflect this verse:

> Give instruction to a wise man, and he will be yet wiser; teach a righteous man—one upright and in right standing with God—and he will increase in learning. (Proverbs 9:9 AMP)

But where can wisdom be found? . . . It cannot be bought with the finest gold, nor can its price be weighed in silver. . . . The fear of the Lord—that is wisdom.

—Proverbs 28:12, 15, 28

Are Bass the Smartest Fish Around?

You see them all the time—bumper stickers that say, "My Child Is the Honor Student of the Month at Davey Elementary School," or "This Car Contains the Parent of an Honor Roll Student," or "Straight-A Student Rides in This Car."

Sometimes you get the feeling the stickers are saying "My Kid Is Smarter Than Your Kid."

I guess I'm waiting for the new fish bumper stickers: "My Fish Is Smarter Than Your Fish," "Bass Are at the Top End of the Smart Gene Pool," or "Bass Think, Trout Swim, and All Others Can't Do Either." Farfetched? Not really. Many anglers believe the fish they go after is smarter than all the other species. Trout anglers go on and on about the legendary smarts of a trout. Bass anglers say the minds of a largemouth and a smallmouth put all others to shame. And would you believe carp (that's right, carp!) anglers see bass and trout as the airhead species? If SAT exams were given to fish, carp enthusiasts think their fish would run mental rings around all other species.

So who's right? Fish IQ tests don't abound. This isn't the easiest question to answer. There was *one* experiment that was both interesting and showed some variation of fish smarts. Eleven species participated in this study. They were bluegill, northern pike, yellow perch, largemouth bass, smallmouth bass, spotted bass, striped bass, bigmouth buffalo, common carp, and channel catfish.

Now it's time for *you* to guess:

1. Which species came out in first place?
2. Which were in the top four?
3. Which came out at the bottom of the smarts?

Here's the experiment: A fish was placed in a tank with a divider and small electric lights. A light close to the fish was switched on for twenty seconds followed by a mild electrical shock if the fish didn't swim over the divider. But if he did swim over the divider in the time allotted, no shock was given and he received a positive score. (Can you see a cheering section for all this?) After several seconds of darkness this was repeated. Each fish went through the exercise twenty-four times on the first day. For the next four to five days each was tested twelve times. The positive—or correct— responses were tabulated and ranked. This was really just a simple avoidance experiment, but it showed a difference in the learning abilities of fish. Now, before you call in for your smart fish bumper stickers, note the results:

Largemouth and smallmouth bass were not the smartest (bummer)! But they weren't the dimmest light bulbs in the chandelier either. They didn't do great but were not bad. Hey, we know they learn. Just toss the same lure at them again and again or use what everyone else is throwing—they figure it out real fast!

Who took top honors? Fortunately, it was a bass. Striped at that. I wish we could stop there, but (groan) the next three (keep this quiet, will you?) were the channel catfish, the bigmouth buffalo, and the common carp. A carp smarter than a largemouth or smallmouth? Our fish just have a greater tolerance for pain ... that's it.

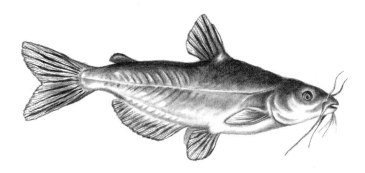

The three on the low end (in descending order) were the northern pike, bluegill, and bringing up the bottom, the yellow perch.[11]

But there's good news in all of this. We've got to be smarter than the bass we're after. Even so, the more we know and the greater our skill the better chance we have to outsmart them. We need to do our homework.

Knowledge and skill give us an edge over a bass. In life,

however, there's another factor that's more important than knowledge and skill. It's called wisdom, and the Bible has much to say about it.

I've seen a number of smart people who lack wisdom. Like the angler who could give you the monthly lunar tables or the structural details of each bass rod available, but who didn't know enough to heed the storm warnings and wondered why his boat swamped in eight-foot waves.

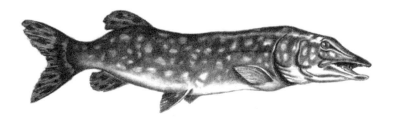

Or the guy who was a genius in his field of mathematical analysis and computers but continued to stand in his boat holding a graphite rod while everyone else fled to the nearest shore to avoid lightning strikes. The difference is being wise.

Do you know what wisdom means? It's the power of judging rightly and following the best course of action. And it's based on knowledge, experience, and understanding. Some have learned to be wise on their own, but there's another type of wisdom that's the best yet. It's not relying on your own wisdom. It comes from another source:

"If any of you lacks wisdom, he should ask God, who gives generously to all without finding fault, and it will be given to him" (James 1:5).

"It is because of him that you are in Christ Jesus, who has become for us wisdom from God—that is—our righteousness, holiness and redemption" (1 Corinthians 1:30). In the Good News Bible, this verse reads, "But God has brought you into union with Christ Jesus, and God has made Christ to be our wisdom."

Charles Swindoll gives an insightful definition to this word: "Wisdom is the God-given ability to see life with rare objectivity and to handle life with rare stability."[12] Now, wouldn't you like to have that in your everyday life? You can. Just ask the right source.

Each creature performs a foreordained function that benefits nature and glorifies God.

—Gary Richmond

God Created Bass, but Why Mosquitoes and Flies?

17

We were standing on a dock, two hundred miles north of the United States border in Saskatchewan, Canada, waiting for our guide to arrive for the day's pike fishing. We'd boated over fifty pike the day before. They weren't the only creatures that were aggressively hungry. So were the mosquitoes! They swarmed around us on the dock. And they were sending out signals to their buddies to come and join in the feast.

My frustration level was at its limit, so I whipped out a mosquito net hat, unfolded it and in the same motion pulled it over my head to get some relief. My fishing partner looked at me and said, "Man, you did that so fast. I hope the mosquitoes you captured inside the net appreciate the meal they're going to have." He was right. In my haste I ended up with several of those pesky creatures inside rather than out. They were in hog heaven until I got rid of them. That was the first problem with the mosquito net. The second occurred a few minutes later when my nose began to run. Without thinking I whipped out my handkerchief and blew my nose . . . right through the mosquito net. It was not a pleasant sight.

Fishing would be so much better if we didn't have to contend with all the bugs like mosquitoes and flies—especially those black flies that seem to have jaws like a snapping turtle. Many have had the delight of what could have been a great fishing experience tarnished by the constant battling with mosquitoes and flies.

In the spring of 2000, we experienced some kind of infestation of minute flies—millions of them—that would settle on all of the boats at the dock. One day we hit a school of small bass that seemed to bite everything we threw at them. In the excitement and frenzy of hitting a jumper on every cast, we'd forget about the bugs and start yelling or breathing with our mouths open—bad idea. We'd inhale a mouthful of these flies. The only way we could avoid this was to speak through clenched teeth!

Have you had an experience where you spent more of your time fighting flies or mosquitoes than enjoying the fishing? It's a part of our pastime. But sometimes you wonder. I can see why God created fish, and especially bass, but some of these insects . . . Why do they have to be around? Some people actually believe that God created mosquitoes and flies to punish and harass us because we are all sinners. I don't think so. A friend of mine, Gary Richmond, who used to work in the veterinary department of the Los Angeles Zoo, said it well:

> It is both comforting and disturbing to know that God created everything for a specific purpose. Nothing was an accident; nothing was unplanned. Not one of the 4.4 million creatures that fly, walk, swim, crawl, wriggle, slide, or hop the earth was a joke or an afterthought. Everything does something that makes its own existence worthwhile. Each creature performs a foreordained function that benefits nature and glorifies God.[13]

In Ecclesiastes 3:14 we read, "I know that everything God does will endure forever; nothing can be added to it and nothing taken from it." When God created the earth and all the animals, it was complete.

Did you know that mosquitoes actually pollinate as many flowers as do bees? Mosquitoes also are a food source for birds. They cause deer herds to migrate to higher country. As the deer move upward to get away from mosquitoes, they prune the lower branches of trees, allowing light to penetrate to the new growth of grasses and plants near the base of those trees. And the deer also fertilize as they feed in these areas.

What about flies? What good is there in this small irritant? They lay eggs that turn into maggots. Maggots were used up to 1932 by doctors to clean up decaying flesh. Flies consume and then eliminate. Plants absorb the flies' waste for their food source. Flies themselves are a major food source for many animals.

So the next time the insects bother you (and they will), remember Genesis 1:24–25, "And God said, 'Let the land produce living creatures according to their kinds: livestock, creatures that move along the ground, and wild animals, each according to its kind.' And it was so. God made the wild animals according to their kinds, the livestock according to their kinds, and all the creatures that move along the ground according to their kinds. And God saw that it was good."

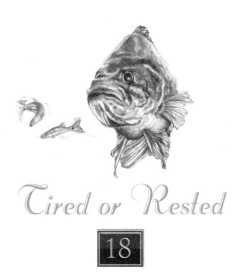

Tired or Rested

18

Have you ever caught a tired bass? Really. Bass can get tired out. Sometimes it's from chasing down those bait fish. It may be they've been carousing all night. Females get tired from their spawning activities. Sometimes a bass is exhausted because an angler played him too long and too hard and kept him out of the water too long. I've watched anglers play and play a bass until there's no energy left in any fin and he's belly up and lethargic when he gets to the boat. That's mistreatment.

Not only do anglers mistreat bass, I've seen them mistreat their rods, reels, boats, lures . . . You name it, they mistreat it—including themselves.

I see it and I hear it. One man told me, "I'm so tired I'm not even sure I want to go out fishing today." When I asked what he had been doing, he replied, "I've been getting up at 3:30 every morning this week to come out fishing. It's my vacation and I want to get the most out of every day. When I'm at work I'm on a six-day, twelve-hour-a-day schedule, and I don't have any free time. And even if I did, I'm too tired to want to do anything."

Have you ever been that tired? Most of us have. It's easy to get too involved and do too much at work, home, church, and even fishing. Some say yes to every request and every opportunity. "No" is not a part of their vocabulary.

Some do too much because they're workaholics.

Some do too much because they build their identities on how much they accomplish.

Some do too much because of ignorance. They believe a Christian always has to be busy.

I talk to a number in counseling who are tired physically. When that happens it creates a domino effect. Soon you're tired emotionally, and you have less control over your emotions and experience greater mood swings. Then you're tired mentally. You're not as sharp and tend to forget little, but important, things. In time you're tired spiritually. You're going through the spiritual motions, but often it's out of obligation and not from the heart.

Sometimes we're tired because we worry. When we worry, there is no rest. Worry is going over something again and again in our mind, reliving what happened or pre-imaging what may occur. It's asking the question "What if?" a dozen times and answering it with greater detail each time. And too often this occurs when we're trying to sleep. We worry about what we have, how to keep it, or get more of what we don't have. "The sleep of a laborer is sweet, whether he eats little or much, but the abundance of a rich man permits him no sleep" (Ecclesiastes 5:12).

Is worry keeping you tired?

> Therefore, prepare your minds for action; be self-controlled; set your hope fully on the grace to be given you when Jesus Christ is revealed. (1 Peter 1:13)
>
> Don't worry about anything; instead, pray about everything; tell God your needs, and don't forget to thank him for his answers. (Philippians. 4:6 TLB)

It's much better to let your mind recover with these principles found in Scripture than to let your mind wear you out.

It may help to ask yourself, "Why am I *doing* all that I'm *doing*?" Much of our life is focused on doing. Jesus said, "Come to me, all you who are weary and burdened, and I will give you rest. Take my yoke upon you and learn from me, for I am gentle and humble in heart, and you will find rest for your souls" (Matthew 11:28–29).

We're interested in our *doing*. God is interested in our rest. When we rest, it's part of the process of coming alive spiritually. Read the following each day. It will do wonders:

> He gives strength to the weary and increases the power of the weak. Even youths grow tired and weary, and young men stumble and fall; but those who hope in the Lord will renew their strength. They will soar on wings like eagles; they will run and not grow weary, they will walk and not be faint. (Isaiah 40:29–31)

Let us run with perseverance the race marked out for us.

—Hebrews 12:1

You've Got to Be Persistent

19

We arrived at the Thornton lakes early in the morning. This was a new experience—fishing several private ponds on a ranch near Gadsden, Alabama. We dropped the boat into one of the ponds, and while listening to stories of all the large bass taken from this impound we began to throw lures and spinnerbaits. We worked around every tree, snag, and brush pile in that pond a couple of times but action was slow. So we came to shore and walked to some other brush-covered ponds. We cast again and again. Finally one fisherman hit a couple of small bass. I began to wonder if this was going to be one of those times when you hear "You should have been here yesterday. We killed them all day long."

We made our way up to the last pond and once again walked the shoreline. I'd caught just a couple, but this other fellow had a dozen or so. When I walked past him I noticed his spinnerbait. It was the same, but it was different. He had a chartreuse trailer bait attached. I dug through my supplies, but I didn't have any. I just ripped the tail off a chartreuse grub, put it on, and cast. The water exploded. The second cast did the same. We all walked around the pond once and decided to bring the boat to this one. For the next three hours we cast those spinnerbaits with trailers and hit fish after fish. We ended up with over sixty, and during the last hour of the day my fishing partner landed the largest bass he'd ever caught. Persistence paid off. You have to have it if you're going to catch bass.

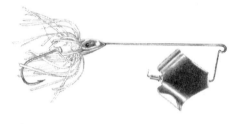

In Chuck Swindoll's book *Come Before Winter*, he talks about the value of persistence in our life:

> How many military battles would never have been won without persistence? How many men and women would never have graduated from school ... or changed careers midstream ... or stayed together in marriage ... or reared a retarded child? Think of the criminal cases that never would have been solved without the relentless persistence of detectives. How about the great music that would never have been finished, the grand pieces of art that would never have graced museums, cathedrals, and monuments the world over? Behind the impeccable beauty of each work is a dream that wouldn't die mixed with the dogged determination of a genius of whom this indifferent world is not worthy.
>
> Think also of the speeches, the sermons, the books that have shaped thinking, infused new hope, prompted fresh faith,

and aroused the will to win. For long and lonely hours away from the applause—even the *awareness*—of the public, the one preparing that verbal missile persisted all alone with such mundane materials as dictionary, thesaurus, historical volumes, biographical data, and a desk full of other research works. The same could be said of those who labor to find cures for diseases. And how about those who experiment with inventions?[14]

Speaking of inventions, if Thomas Edison hadn't been persistent you and I would be in the dark . . . literally. He and his helpers kept at it. One of them said, "What a waste. We've tried seven hundred experiments and nothing has worked. We're no better off than when we started."

But Edison said, "Oh yes, we are; we know seven hundred things that *won't* work. We're closer than we've ever been before."

You know, God honors our persistence. He's also persistent in pursuing us.

> And I am convinced and sure of this very thing, that He Who began a good work in you will continue until the day of Jesus Christ—right up to the time of His return—developing [that good work] and perfecting and bringing it to full completion. (Philippians 1:6 AMP)

Character is the weight beneath our waterline.

Character

20

"𝓜an, is he a character!"

"What a character. You never know what he's going to do next."

You've probably said it about someone else or someone has called you a character. Some of the most colorful characters I've seen are out fishing or on those TV fishing shows. Some guys are a delight to be around. Others are grumpy and sullen. I've even heard bass referred to as characters. One new angler I took out referred to every bass that jumped as a real character, especially the one he released that jumped back up and tried to hit his lure two feet out of the water.

Often we use *character* to refer to someone who's a bit odd or different. It can also mean a distinctive trait, quality, or attribute. Another meaning is a pattern of behavior or personality. Character is what we're really made of—what we're like when life takes a turn for the worse.

Several years ago Michael Plant, one of the world's best yachtsmen, purchased a state-of-the-art sailboat with the best navigational equipment money could buy. On this boat, *The Coyote*, was an emergency global positioning locator. With the press of a button, the system would transmit a signal that would be picked up by satellite. Within a few seconds, either of two ground locations could pinpoint Plant's coordinates, even in the middle of the vast ocean. *The Coyote* was the most fail-safe vessel of its kind.

Early in the fall of 1992, Plant set out from the East Coast on a solo voyage to France. On the fourth day of the journey, ground locators lost contact with *The Coyote*. Weather scans of the Atlantic showed storms causing high seas, so it was assumed that Plant was navigating the storms and would soon regain contact. But he never did.

Search-and-rescue squads were deployed to the last known location of *The Coyote*, but no sign was found. Commercial airliners were asked to monitor their emergency channels in case Plant was broadcasting signals for help.

Two weeks after his departure, a ship about four hundred miles off the Azores came upon the sailboat floating upside down.

Hoisting *The Coyote* up for a closer look, the rescuers searched the cabin, hoping to find the emergency life raft already deployed, which would indicate that Michael Plant might still be alive in the Atlantic. But they found the life raft only partially inflated, still stuck in the hull of the boat. His body was never found.

The telltale culprit in the accident was a broken keel. No one knows why, but the ballast had been broken off, leaving the boat without any weight in the keel. The ballast was an eight-thousand-pound weight placed in the keel, making this sailboat one of the safest vessels on the ocean. Because of the amount of weight in the keel, even should it capsize, the design of the ballast would roll it upright again. Yet without weight in the keel, *The Coyote* was no match for the Atlantic storms.

To have stability in a storm, there must be *more weight beneath the waterline than above it.* Without it, a boat can look fine in the bay or in calm water. As someone said, "Ships are safe in the harbor, but that's not what ships were made for."

Character is the weight beneath our waterline. Without it, we may look good in the harbor. We can fly our colors and strut our stuff, but we will be no match for the currents. Storms don't only develop character, they *reveal* it.

Everyone has character. But here's a different way of looking at it:

> Therefore since we have been justified through faith, we have peace with God through our Lord Jesus Christ, through whom we have gained access by faith into this grace in which we now stand. And we rejoice in the hope of the glory of God. Not only so, but we also rejoice in our sufferings, because we know that suffering produces perseverance; perseverance, character; and character, hope. (Romans 5:1–4)

If you want not only to *be* a character but also to *have* character, there's just one way to do it. Paul said, "So I tell you: Live by following the Spirit ... [who] produces the fruit of love, joy, peace, patience, kindness, goodness, faithfulness, gentleness, self-control" (Galatians 5:16, 22–23 NCV).

If these qualities are a consistent part of your life, you really will be different in today's world. So if someone says you're odd or eccentric because of this, be thankful.

*Blessed is the man [whose]
delight is in the law of the Lord,
and on his law he meditates day
and night. He is like a tree planted
by streams of water, which yields
its fruit in season and whose leaf
does not wither. Whatever he does
prospers.*

—Psalm 1:1–3

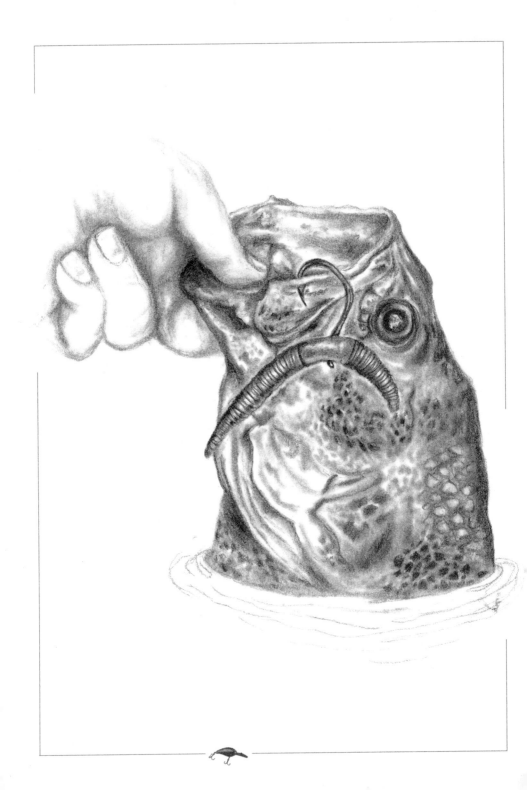

Anger and Fishing Don't Mix

21

An angry angler is no fun to be around. Sometimes you get stuck with one in your boat, or his boat stops ten feet away from you and the waves just about swamp your boat. I've seen angry anglers ram their boat into a dock. Another berated his small son in front of others for losing a fish. I've seen guides become angry at clients for not catching their instructions the first time around. I remember taking a group of married couples on an outing on the Snake River in Grand Teton National Park. For some it was the first time they'd ever fished. One of the wives caught several beautifully colored Yellowstone cutthroat trout. She was delighted. Her husband was angry. Instead of enjoying his wife's catch with her, he was resentful. What's your anger style? Patrick Morley had some insights about three angry men:

> *Freddie Flash* has a short fuse. It doesn't take much to set him off. Because he has such a low flash point, he loses his temper too often. His anger problem is a *frequency* problem. Some of his friends have been heard to say, "Freddie is mad at the world."
>
> Minor irritations blow way out of proportion to Freddie. He is an angry man looking for a place to be angry, exploding

at the slightest provocation, though his anger subsides just as quickly. He thinks the harm he does is inconsequential. It hasn't dawned on him that it's not the single occurrence but the frequency that has branded him as someone to avoid.

Cary Control doesn't become angry every day. But, boy-oh-boy, when Cary's long fuse finally burns down, the dynamite explodes! He loses control and strikes out with a verbal tirade that makes his wife's knees wobble and his children flinch in terror. His anger problem is an *intensity* problem.

Gary Grudge never has an outburst of anger. Instead, Gary seethes with anger and plots his revenge. His counterattacks are designed to discredit the man he hates. Gary often wakes in the middle of the night, a cold sweat reminding him of the one who has done him wrong. His anger problem is a problem of *duration*.

As a grudge-holder, the toxic juices of anger burn on the lining of his stomach wall like rust-remover on an old corroded hinge. He feeds his ulcer the right foods, but his high blood pressure and colitis require a doctor's prescription.

Anger destroys the quality of our personal lives, our marriages, and our health. Angry words are like irretrievable arrows released from an archer's bow. Once released, traveling through the air toward their target, they cannot be withdrawn, their damage cannot be undone. Like the arrows of the archer, our angry words pierce like a jagged blade, ripping at the heart of their target.[15]

You may want to remember these words.

Don't make friends with quick-tempered people or spend time with those who have bad tempers. If you do, you will be like them. Then you will be in real danger. (Proverbs 22:24–25 NCV)

When you are angry, do not sin, and be sure to stop being angry before the end of the day. (Ephesians 4:26 NCV)

My grace is sufficient for you, for power is perfected in weakness.

—2 Corinthians 12:9 NASB

Unraveled

22

$\mathcal{I}$ was sitting in a boat at the dock waiting for a friend to show up. I looked up and saw a large pickup pull in towing a large boat that seemed a bit out of place for the type of fishing we did at this small impound. It wasn't so much the length but the depth and width. The boat had a big center console with a large steering wheel and several rods attached to it in an upright position. This craft would have looked more at home on the ocean than in this lake.

As the driver backed the boat down the ramp into the water, another fellow hopped in the boat and grabbed a rod to begin getting ready. I heard him say, "What the ... Hey, there's no line on this reel I filled just last night!"

The two talked it over and realized that while they were driving along the freeway the line must have come loose and slowly begun to unwind until it was all gone. They'd been spooled! Can you imagine driving along behind them at sixty-five miles an hour, and you begin to see a thin line dancing around your windshield, wrapping itself around your windshield wipers or antenna? Someone probably discovered that line.

Fortunately, these two men could laugh about their experience and refill the reel.

Sometimes we feel like that reel. We've been spooled. We want life to go smoothly (the way we want it) and it doesn't. Our plans and dreams unravel, and whereas life was good, now it's upset. It's a backlash right when the bass are tearing into a school of shad on the surface, or a nut falling off your reel into the lake.

Life can unravel in other ways too.

Perhaps you can remember a significant day in baseball. One of the best hitters for the Montreal Expos was at the plate facing a hard-throwing pitcher for the San Francisco Giants. The pitcher looked at the runner at first base and then threw as hard as he could. Little did he know it was the last pitch he would ever throw in any kind of game. A sharp crack was heard throughout the stadium as the bone in Dave Dravecky's arm snapped in two. Those watching saw him grasp his arm, scream, and fall to the ground. Later he said he'd felt like his arm was going to fly toward home plate.

It wasn't just that his arm was broken. The doctors found that the cancer he thought was in remission had reappeared. The arm would have to be amputated at the shoulder to ensure the cancer wouldn't spread to the rest of his body.

I think of a friend of mine who was driving home from work when he came upon an accident. A car had hit a motorcycle. My friend stopped and went over to the car to see if the occupants were all right. They were. He then walked toward the downed motorcycle and felt a subtle sense of recognition. As he stepped over the green motorcycle and lifted the visor of the rider's helmet, he recognized the face of his nineteen-year-old son, who was dead.

Those who survive are people with faith, especially faith in the promises of God. Dwell on His promises. Believe them:

Blessed are those who mourn, for they will be comforted. (Matthew 5:4)

Come to me, all you who are weary and heavy-laden, and I will give you rest. (Matthew 11:28)

Blessed be the God and Father of our Lord Jesus Christ, the Father of mercies and God of all comfort; who comforts us in all our affliction. (2 Corinthians 1:3–4 RSV)

When you pass through the waters, I will be with you; and through the rivers, they will not overflow you. When you walk through the fire, you will not be scorched, nor will the flame burn you. (Isaiah 43:2 NASB)

And in the same way the Spirit also helps our weakness; for we do not know how to pray as we should, but the Spirit Himself intercedes for us with groanings too deep for words. (Romans 8:26 NASB)

For I am convinced that neither death, nor life, nor angels, nor principalities, nor things present, nor things to come, nor powers, nor height, nor depth, nor any other created thing, shall be able to separate us from the love of God, which is in Christ Jesus our Lord. (Romans 8:38–39 NASB)

*C*ast your cares on the Lord and
he will sustain you; he will never
let the righteous fall.

—*Psalm 55:22*

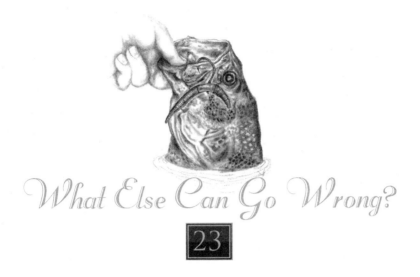

What Else Can Go Wrong?

23

$\mathcal{A}$ friend and I were on our way to Silverwood Lake, in southern California, for a couple of days. We rented an old cabin, and the next morning I began to cook breakfast. I tossed the bacon in the pan, took out a can of frozen OJ, opened it, and the entire contents hit the floor with a loud, gooey splat. I grabbed some paper towels to wipe it up, but the goo just seemed to spread. I got more towels and was so intent on cleaning up the mess, I forgot the bacon. That is, until the smoke alarm went off. My friend Phil yelled, "Need some help?"

My response was, "Nope, I've got it under control," and I tossed the OJ and bacon with all its grease into the trash. We finally ate, and while Phil washed dishes I picked up the big brown paper sack of trash, opened the front door, and stopped dead in my tracks. My 1973 four-door Plymouth with a sixteen-foot aluminum boat on its paisley roof had a flat tire. Just when I was thinking *What else can go wrong?* it did!

The bottom of the trash bag with the OJ concentrate and bacon gave way and everything dropped out . . . right onto my feet. Phil came outside and saw what had happened, almost made a comment, but—fortunately for him—wisdom prevailed. We got out the spare that was half flat, put it on the car, and then drove around for an hour looking for a gas station for air.

That accomplished, we drove twenty minutes down the backside of the mountain range to the lake, parked, got out, and went to take the boat off the car. Now, you need to know that I was safety conscious; I didn't want anyone stealing this boat, so I had locked it with a large chain and a Master padlock. The chain went through one of the struts on the boat and through the car door handle. When I put my hand in my pocket for the key, a picture formed in my mind: the keys were on the table back at the cabin.

That's right. Old "I can do it myself" had left the keys behind. I wasn't about to drive back, so we got out the tools, took the strut off the boat, got the boat off the car roof, and went fishing. I don't know what others thought as they looked at this car sitting in the parking lot with a huge chain padlocked to a door handle and nothing else! I don't want to know. It was one of "those" days.

When was the last time you had one of those fur-ball rotten days? A day where nothing seems to go well: people are late, they don't follow through, dinner is cold, everyone wants something from you with no real appreciation of your effort, the expressway is a mess, and nothing you do turns out right! You're irritated and discouraged.

When days like this occur, sometimes we compound the

problem by making one major mistake—we try to fix everything by ourselves. That's what I did. We take on the role of the Lone Ranger and tough it out alone. But even the Lone Ranger was smart enough to have a partner.

This is the time to say "God, help me" and He will. One of the best ways to handle these days is to dwell on God's Word. Read these passages out loud during your dark days. Reflect on what each one says, and then note the difference it makes in your attitude toward the day.

> I have set the Lord always before me. Because he is at my right hand, I will not be shaken. (Psalm 16:8)
>
> You, O Lord, keep my lamp burning; my God turns my darkness into light. (Psalm 18:28)
>
> The Lord is my light and my salvation—whom shall I fear? The Lord is the stronghold of my life—of whom shall I be afraid? (Psalm 27:1)
>
> God is our refuge and strength, an ever-present help in trouble. (Psalm 46:1)
>
> Create in me a pure heart, O God, and renew a steadfast spirit within me. (Psalm 51:10)
>
> My soul finds rest in God alone; my salvation comes from him. (Psalm 62:1)

*Always give thanks for everything
to our God and Father in the
name of our Lord Jesus Christ.*

—*Ephesians 5:20* TLB

Don't Take It for Granted

24

$\mathcal{I}$magine you're out on a lake with small sheltered coves. You need to get in close without spooking those bass that are up shallow. You have two ways to get your boat close enough. Either crank up your 175-horsepower motor or get out the oars. Neither option is high on your list. But it's all you've got.

You're probably thinking, *"Wrong, Norm. I'll just use my trolling motor."* But guess again. Trolling motors were never invented. What? Well, not really. But can you imagine a day on the lake without one? Imagine what it would be like if trolling motors *were* never invented. We take them for granted, but it would be inconvenient without one on our boat. A trolling motor makes maneuvering easy and frees up our hands and brains to fish.

What do you know about trolling motors? Were they invented before World War II? World War I? How about before the Spanish-

American War? Frenchman Gustave Trouce constructed the first one in 1881. You can imagine how wild it looked. Although it was awkward, it worked well enough to steer a small skiff. Steam power now had a competitor—electric power. But when gas motors appeared in the late 1890s development slowed down. By 1920 it looked as though the gas outboard had wiped out the electric motor. If that had happened . . . what a tragedy!

But in the 1930s a North Dakota man developed a lightweight, efficient motor for his own use. His friends pressured him for more. So using a Model A Ford starter engine that was mounted  out of the water, the Minn Kota came into being. And over the decades the motor as well as production methods were refined.

In the 1940s a man from Mississippi built his own version. But he took it one step further (literally); he didn't like the clumsy, distracting steering by hand, so he blessed all of us with a little device that made steering and fishing so much easier—the foot pedal. Because his final product took the place of a human guide, he called it (you guessed it) the motor guide.

Over the years the trolling motors have evolved: permanent magnet motors in place of field-wound motors, variable speed controls, a folding bracket to stow the motor when running the boat, greater thrust, and eventually the weldless prop . . . and talk about power. There's one that produces 165-pound thrust on twenty-four volts. (That's everything you need to know about electric motors—or didn't want to know!)

So the next time you use your electric motor, don't take it for granted. Imagine your day without it![16]

Trolling motors aren't the only things that we take for granted and would be up a creek without. Can you imagine what your life would be like if you didn't have a Bible in your own language, or if it were against the law to have one? Or if you couldn't worship God openly—as happens in some countries today? (How many times have we missed a worship service because of . . . oh, well, let's not go there!)

But worst of all, what if God had never sent His Son, Jesus, to die for our sins and bridge the gap between Him and us. What would this life be like? Can you imagine life without Jesus? Can you imagine eternal life without Him? God, in His Word, calls us to be grateful people. He calls us to be thankful people. Take a moment and list all that you have because of God's goodness. Go ahead. It will help you get a new perspective on life.

I will meditate upon [your words] and give them my full respect. I will delight in them and not forget them.... Open my eyes to see wonderful things in your Word.

—Psalm 119:15–16, 18 TLB

I Hooked Him!

25

You cast that top-water lure next to a half-submerged log and let it sit there for a minute, letting all the ripples subside, and then give it a slight twitch. The water explodes as a bass erupts from underneath and you slam that rod up to set the hook. He takes off and then decides to go airborne. But he's not the only airborne object—the lure pulled loose and it's flying back on a direct line for your head unless you duck. You value your life so you duck, but as that lure with all the hooks flies past, you wonder, *What went wrong? I thought I set the hook. Something's wrong with the hooks.* You know what? You could be right, and it could be the hooks weren't sharp enough or the barbs had broken off.

Unfortunately, some anglers treat their hooks like second-class citizens. They're tossed in a box, allowed to dull and rust, and they fall into disrepair. Perhaps it's time to take an inventory of the hooks in your tackle box. The selection available to a bass angler today is never ending. You can choose the following styles from Gamakatsu: EWG Treble, Extra-Wide Gap Worm, Light Wire Worm, 60° Hook, or Octopus Bronze. From Mustad you could choose: Ultra Point Impact Keeper, Demon Circle, Mega-Bite, or Mega-Lite. (If you would like to check these out—or dozens of others—take a look at a Bass Pro Shops catalog.)

And if your hook isn't sharp, you won't hook that ol' gristle-mouth bass.

What do you know about hooks? After all, isn't a hook just a hook? Aren't they like those old tube socks—one size fits all? Definitely not.

There is a hook science. When you select a hook there are three considerations—hooking power, holding power, and how the weight or shape of the hook affects the lure or bait to which it's connected. What impacts these three? The point and barb design, metal quality or stiffness, and shank length and diameter. You can now purchase fluorescent, phosphorescent, or lacquered hooks. Brilliant concept![17]

Let's take the "hook" test.

1. What are the seven parts of a hook's basic anatomy? Describe them.
2. What's a straight-shank hook and its basic purpose?
3. What's an offset-shank hook and its basic purpose?
4. How would you describe a bait-saver hook and how it compares to a circle hook?

Are you ready for the answers? For question 1, if you said eye, shank, gap, throat, bend, barb, and point, you got 'em all. But did you describe them? Most know what the eye, point, and barb are, but the gap and the throat? The gap is the distance between the tip of the point and the shank measured in a straight line. The throat is the distance between the bend at its deepest point and the gap.

(2) A straight-shank hook has a head angle known as a "sproat bend." Near the eye are tiny barbs that hold soft plastic baits snuggly. It's used for plastic worms, lizards, and small finesse lives.

(3) The offset-shank hook is just that—it has an offset shank by the eye to hold the head of a plastic worm or other offering so it doesn't slide on the shaft during the cast or a bite.

(4) A bait-saver hook is a wide-gap hook with a thin, barbed stud attached to the hook-eye for Texas-rigging. This makes hook setting easier. This differs from the circle hook in that the circle has an offset "hangnail" point that tends to result in more lip hooking rather than gut hooking, thus easier to release your fish.

No matter what hooks you use, always check them. Quality hooks should come super sharp. Even then, it helps to carry a fine-grain file especially made to sharpen hooks.[18]

The more you know about the variety of hooks, as well as regularly checking and maintaining them, the better equipped you will be.

It's like living the Christian life. The more we know about our faith, the Word of God, and Jesus Christ, the more likely we are to have a Christian walk that's productive and fulfilling. But just like keeping our hooks sharp, we need to pay attention to our relationship with Jesus.

I'm sure you spend time sharpening your hooks. What could

you do to sharpen your faith? It may be time to do an inventory in this area of your life as well. And the results *will* be better than landing that double-digit bass!

Have You Ever Fallen?

26

It's embarrassing. There's no other word for it. You're just walking along and you either trip over your feet or miss a step and splat! You fall on your face. If any of your friends are around to see it, you know what you're going to hear about the rest of the day!

Years ago I was trout fishing with some friends on the Madison River near Ennis, Montana. It was a beautiful, clear day, and as I walked along the bank I noticed an island with some deep pools alongside it. They just had to be filled with fish. So I began wading across the river. The water wasn't overly deep, but the bottom was covered with rounded, slippery rocks. I was careful and made it across. I was right. The fish were there and hungry. From time to time a raft floated by filled with people either fishing or just enjoying the float trip.

About an hour later I was ready to wade back. For some reason the current seemed a bit stronger. I was concerned about slipping on the rocks and was especially cautious when I looked upstream and saw a raft on its way. If I fell, I didn't want it to happen in front of all those people. That would be embarrassing and, worse yet, they were probably armed with video cameras. So I waited, and we waved to one another as they glided past. When I didn't think they could see me, I took my first step—on a rounded rock that gave way. I slipped and fell in. My bottom bounced off the river bottom, and since my eyes were open I looked up and could see the surface. I thrust downward with my feet and came upright with my arms in the air clutching my rod. Actually, that's what I cared about. I didn't want to lose it. I looked around. No one saw me. Yes! That, too, was important. I kept wading, got across, and was none the worse for wear from my fall.

At many camps and conference grounds throughout the country there's a new activity. They call it *The Wall*. It's a fifty-foot simulated rock climb, a wall of wood with rock-shaped fingerholds jutting out all over. But this one is safe. Around your waist you wear a harness that's attached to a rope running through a pulley. Someone holds onto the rope and secures it for you as you climb. If your fingers and hands tire and you happen to fall (which happens to many), the rope saves you.

It's a good metaphor for life, because we fall in other ways, too. Our hands have slipped from promises, commitments, and even convictions. Max Lucado describes what happens after we fall:

> Now you are wiser. You have learned to go slowly. You are careful. You are cautious, but you are also confident. You trust

the rope. You rely on the harness. And though you can't see your guide, you know him. You know he is strong. You know he is able to keep you from falling.

And you know you are only a few more steps from the top. So whatever you do, don't quit. Though your falls are great, his strength is greater. You will make it. You will see the summit. You will stand at the top. And when you get there, the first thing you'll do is join with all the others who have made the climb and sing this verse:

"To him who is able to keep you from falling . . ."[19]

To him who is able to keep you from falling and to present you before his glorious presence without fault and with great joy—to the only God our Savior be glory, majesty, power and authority, through Jesus Christ our Lord, before all ages, now and forevermore! Amen. (Jude 24–25)

No temptation has seized you except what is common to man. And God is faithful; he will not let you be tempted beyond what you can bear. But when you are tempted, he will also provide a way out so that you can stand up under it. (1 Corinthians 10:13)

Every loss is important. It is part of life and cannot be avoided.

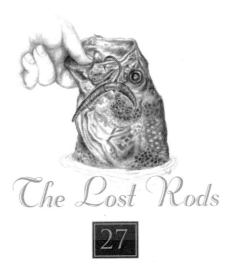

The Lost Rods

27

$\mathcal{G}$o ahead, you can admit it. If you've fished for a while you've lost a fishing rod, or two or three. The experience is not one we want to repeat. But it happens to the best of us. The only thing worse is when you're showing your friends and relatives how far your rod will bend and not break . . . and it breaks! Yup, when I was fourteen that's exactly what I did, but that was before fiber glass, graphite, and all the other components.

Do you remember the first rod you lost? Think back to where, how . . . and what you said! If it hasn't occurred, it will.

Once I was trout fishing in the Buffalo River in Grand Teton National Park. I was in the river, got my line snagged on a log, and it broke just when the second section of the two-part rod came undone and began sliding down the line. If the lure had been at the end of the line, this piece of the rod would have stopped. But there was no lure. As I watched that rod slide slowly down the line that feeling of powerlessness, dread, and "Oh no!" swept over me. I stood there helpless as the current sped it down the line and then out of sight. I stood there with the butt end of my rod in my hand.

Years later I stood on the dock of a lake casting with a water-filled bubble to get the bait out there 150 feet or more. I decided to let fly to see how far I could cast. So I did. It was a great—no, a tremendous—cast. I put every ounce I had into it and let fly. The bubble and bait flew out there, the line stripped off the reel, and the rod and reel followed. I couldn't believe it . . . I let go of them and watched the rod fly gracefully into the air and then like a Saturn rocket gradually curve until it pointed down and plunged through the surface of the lake. My fishing partner looked over, grunted, and said, "Great cast . . . different . . . but great."

The most recent cast episode involved a new bass rod. It was the first time I'd used it. We were using a trolling motor to get to the other side of the lake, so I thought I'd troll and jig while we were moving. Everything would have gone well had I not put the pole down and braced it under my leg (so I thought) and reached for the thermos. Not only does this lake have a good population of small bass, but just as many large, aggressive catfish who don't understand they're not supposed to hit bass lures. Suddenly one of them hit the spider jig just as I was leaning the wrong way. That rod didn't fall overboard—it took off through the air like a missile shot from a destroyer. We sat there watching that missile, not believing and not wanting to believe what we were seeing. That rod was being towed around the lake somewhere. Perhaps someday I'll catch that cat. Who knows, maybe even the rod. I was not a happy camper.

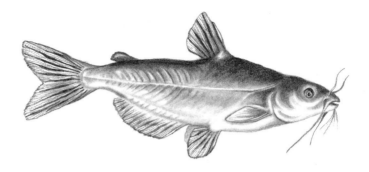

Losing a rod doesn't make for the best day. But there are other losses that leave a hole in your life. You don't recover all that soon. In fact, some losses you never fully recover from.

What have you lost in your life that's impacted you? Some have lost a job. Others have lost a spouse through death or divorce. Perhaps you've lost a child. I did. My profoundly retarded son, Matthew, died at the age of twenty-two. That was in 1990. I still feel it at times. And since he was retarded there were other losses as well. I watched a dad play catch with his son the other day. I felt a stab of loss again. I never got to do that. I never got to fish with Matthew, either. I wish I could have.

So what can we do with a loss in our life? Think about this: Every loss is important. It is part of life and cannot be avoided. Losses are necessary! You grow by losing and then accepting the loss. Change occurs through loss. Growth occurs through loss. Life takes on a deeper and richer meaning because of losses. The better you handle them, the healthier you will be and the more you will grow. No one said that loss was fair, but it is part of life.

Loss can strengthen your faith. It enables you to trust more in

God than in yourself. Every loss allows you to rest in the grace and comfort of God.

It will also produce maturity in your life. Paul talked about this:

> Moreover—let us also be full of joy now! Let us exalt and triumph in our troubles and rejoice in our sufferings, knowing that pressure and affliction and hardship produce patient and unswerving endurance. And endurance (fortitude) develops maturity of character—that is, approved faith and tried integrity. And character [of this sort] produces [the habit of] joyful and confident hope of eternal salvation. (Romans 5:3–4 AMP)

There *is* a purpose in loss. It may not be obvious. Give it time. Your life will be different.

(*Note*: If you have experienced recent serious losses in your life, you may want to read *Recovering From the Losses of Life* by Norm Wright, Baker Book House.)

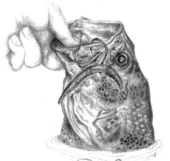

Listen to the Weather Report

28

The weatherman—oops, the *meteorologist*—comes on the air, and you listen intently. "There's a chance of rain with a possible cold front on the horizon. However, it could stay clear for a few days with a few high clouds occasionally." What'd he say? Couldn't he give you a definite maybe? Weather people just don't understand how important weather is to bass fishing. It's critical to locating and catching them.

A cold front coming—words we don't want to hear. It's usually an indication the bass are going to slow down. Do you know what a cold front actually is? It's the line where a mass of cold air hits a mass of hot air and temperatures drop within a few hours.

Bass seem to sense this. It's as though they know feeding opportunities will be cut back after the front comes through so they decide to hit the buffet line while it's still available. Bass swimming in the flats head for the first drop off. Any drop in water temperature causes them to move tight to cover or deeper, and thus their strike zone shrinks. During the fall, you may have the reverse. An early snowstorm can cause a feeding frenzy since the hot water temperature has dropped. The fishing frequently picks up just before the front arrives. But it often takes up to three days for the conditions to get back to normal.

Recently I fished a new lake that seemed to have all sorts of potential. It was a beautifully clear, calm morning with just a bit of a breeze. At noon I came off the water and talked to one of the regulars. He said, "You'll never see it this way again. This lake is known for winds with white caps. So get a good anchor and find a point. These fish love the wind."

Many anglers head for shore when the wind hits. They don't want to fight the elements. But this could be the best time of all. Bass do like the wind. Here are five reasons why you should learn to enjoy it too:

1. The wind causes microscopic plankton to drift and accumulate. So? Baitfish feed on this, get active, and move into windblown banks to feed, which signals the bass, "Come and get us!"
2. Waves churn up leaves and litter on the bottom. Crawdads come out and the bass rejoice.
3. If a lake is clear, waves can create a murky section close to shore. Hungry bass can hang out here looking for food.
4. Waves in hot weather can oxygenate water that is low in oxygen from the heat. This is better for baitfish and bass alike.
5. Wind can create currents in narrow passageways in a lake.

As the baitfish move through these areas, it's easy for the bass to ambush them.

Remember these five positive factors about wind, and cast accordingly.

Let's consider one other weather factor. Do bass hit better on sunny or overcast days? Most think that's a no-brainer: of course it's the overcast days. Perhaps, but guides who go after trophy bass catch the biggest fish on sunny days. Bass tend to be visual feeders, and visibility decreases as the clouds intensify. You can have a great catch on cloudy days if you use large and/or noisy lures. The darker the cloud cover, the better to use the noisier and topwater lures. The finish of your lure is important when the clouds are out. Change from a reflective finish to a flat (bone white) or hot (orange, chartreuse). Let them see your lure.[20]

Bass aren't the only ones affected by the weather. We all have storms and waves come into our lives and churn things up. Some of our sunny days are going to be dimmed by the clouds as well.

That evening, Jesus said to his followers, "Let's go across the lake." Leaving the crowd behind, they took him in the boat just as he was. There were also other boats with them. A very strong wind came up on the lake. The waves came over the sides and into the boat so that it was already full of water. Jesus was at the back of the boat, sleeping with his head on a cushion. His followers woke him and said, "Teacher, don't you care that we are drowning!"

Jesus stood up and commanded the wind and said to the waves, "Quiet! Be still!" Then the wind stopped, and it became completely calm. (Mark 4:35–39 NCV)

The calmness may be Jesus intervening in your circumstances. The calmness may not be intervention in your circumstances, but Jesus giving you the calm and strength to handle the turmoil.

"Don't be afraid, because I have saved you. I have called you by name, and you are mine. When you pass through the waters, I will be with you. When you cross rivers, you will not drown. When you walk through fire, you will not be burned, nor will the flames hurt you." (Isaiah 43:1–2 NCV)

The Fine Art of Fishing– A History

29

$\mathcal{W}$hat do you know about fishing's history? To appreciate the fine art of fishing as it is today, it may help to know the sport's past. For starters,

How did the earliest anglers catch fish?
What was the first hook made of?
What country has the earliest record of fishing with rods?
What's the first fishing match ever described?

If you know the answers, you're a true student of fishing. For the rest of us:
The first anglers in North America caught fish with their hands.

Those who migrated from Europe learned the art of *guddling* from Native Americans. This is slowly moving the hand under the body of a resting wild fish until it could be seized by the gills and yanked from the water. This practice has evolved into a growing sport today, especially with catfish. The first rods probably were sapling branches used to reach less accessible waters.

The first hook was probably not a hook at all; it was a piece of flint or stone that a fish could swallow with the bait, but couldn't spit out. Stone or flint flakes have been found with grooves to hold a line. And some early lures were made of ivory and bone.

From the fourth century B.C., Chinese writings describe fishing with a bamboo rod, a silk line, a hook made from a needle, and for bait? Cooked rice. Egypt has hieroglyphics describing the wealthy class fishing with shorter rods and lines.

What about the first fishing match (or tournament)? Plutarch described one between Anthony and Cleopatra. That would have been interesting.

Fishermen are prominent in Scripture. The image of a fish is used to represent believers. Sites for monasteries in Europe were chosen, in part, around good fishing streams. If none were available, the monks built fishponds, because fish was a mainstay of their diet.

Who wrote the first article on sport fishing? A nun. It's true. Dame Juliana Berners, the Lady Prioress of Sopwell Nunnery, wrote the *Book of St. Albans* in England in 1498. She gave advice on several items including how to make a rod, hooks, and line (at that time it was braided line made from the tail hair of white stallions). She even wrote about conservation.[21]

It seems fishing didn't change much over the years until the twentieth century, and when it did, well, just look at where we are today.

Let's look at history in another way: your life, and in particular your spiritual life. Sometimes our spiritual life stays the same year after year as angling did century after century. Perhaps it needs to be given a boost as angling has experienced in the past fifty years. It may help to look at your activity level in your church as well as your walk with the Lord. Use this chart to help in the process:

My Spiritual History

Years	Number of Activities	Walk With the Lord Rate yourself from 1 to 5: 1 = close; 5 = distant
10 years ago		
9 years ago		
8 years ago		
7 years ago		
6 years ago		
5 years ago		
4 years ago		
3 years ago		

2 years ago

_____

1 year ago

_____

This year

_____

What does this assessment tell you about your spiritual life? Is it in balance, and are you growing? Maybe you've discovered that your spiritual life is in balance; you have set aside appropriate times for personal time with God, and you are energized by involvements. Or, maybe you've discovered that you're doing a lot but are not growing or deepening as a result of your study, service, teaching, or group participation. If you are in the latter category, you may want to back off from what you are doing and reassess your spiritual life. Sometimes people experience spiritual burnout.

Have you ever considered taking a personal retreat? One man took a half-day to reflect on his spiritual life. He spent it in the sanctuary of his church when no one else was around to bother him. He prayed, read Scripture aloud, sang hymns, and sat in various pews. He studied the stained-glass windows, which he noticed in detail for the first time. His prayer was simple: "Lord, draw me closer to you, and show me what you want and don't want me to do."

As you look at what you are involved in, ask the Lord to show you what is important to Him. Ask Him to show you where you need to spend more time or less time.

We Weren't Meant to Live in a Cave

30

𝒜 number of years ago there was a great deal of discussion about the huge brown trout in Flaming Gorge Reservoir in Utah. Much of the talk centered around one angler who was catching ten- to twenty-pound fish one after another. He seemed almost driven in his quest to catch these monster fish. If you fished with him you had to follow his instructions *exactly*. He would fish day after day starting at three A.M. He was married with children, but to devote as much time as he could to fishing, he'd live in a cave for weeks with just the bare necessities—even in the cold early spring.

Can you imagine living in a barren cold cave in a sleeping bag and getting up in the middle of the night to begin trolling? He'd go for days with little or no contact with people. We aren't meant to live in caves. If we do, we end up starving relationally. In his *Mars and Venus* books, John Gray talks about men retreating to their caves rather than working out some of their issues with their wives. We all have our caves. Can you identify yours?

There's a man in the Old Testament who decided to get away from all the hassles and live in a cave for a while. He was depressed and bummed out about everything. A woman made a threat on his life and he quickly forgot how God had used him, how He had overcome the false prophets of Baal and had demonstrated His power in the land. You can read about it in 1 Kings 19. God came to him and ministered to him. He gave him rest and food and talked with him. Elijah recovered and went back to being with people. In fact, God gave him a good friend.

Have you ever felt like getting away from it all—especially people? Have you ever felt so discouraged that you wished you could find a cave and crawl in it and hide? You know, no people, no hassles, no problems. When this happens, sometimes it's self-pity, sometimes depression that is to blame. It can hit any of us, and we  don't want to be around anyone—even some of those at church. Consider what Chuck Swindoll has to say about this:

> God has not designed us to live like hermits in a cave. He has designed us to live in friendship and fellowship and community with others. That's why the church, the body of Christ,

is so very important, for it is there that we are drawn together in love and mutual encouragement. We're meant to be a part of one another's lives. Otherwise, we pull back, focusing on ourselves—thinking about how hard we have it or how unfair others are.

Elijah *had* to get his eyes back on the Lord. That was absolutely essential. He had been used mightily, but it was *the Lord* who made him mighty. He stood strong against the enemy, but it was *the Lord* who had given him the strength.

Often we are more enamored with the gifts God gives us than with the Giver himself. When the Lord brings rest and refreshment, we become more grateful for the rest and refreshment than for the God who allows it. When God gives us a good friend, we become absorbed in that friendship and so preoccupied with the friend that we forget it was our gracious God who gave us the friend. We so easily focus on the wrong things.

We're shut away in our cave of loneliness and discouragement, and then God brings along the gifts of rest and refreshment, wise counsel, and close, personal friends. And we fall in love with the gifts, rather than the Giver!

He gives us a verse of Scripture, and we worship the Bible rather than the One who gave it. He gives us a loving wife or husband or friend, and we fall more in love with the person than the One who gave us that important individual. He gives us a good job, and we love the job more than we love Him. And all He wants is for us to look up to Him and realize "I gave that to you." He longs to have us look up and say, "Oh, thank you, Father! I miss you. I want to be with you."

Elijah reminds us to look up. Don't focus on what He gives, focus on Him.

Let's look up after the Lord graciously delivers us from our depression.

Let's look up when He allows us rest and refreshment following an exhausting schedule that has taken its toll on us.

Let's look up and thank Him when He gently and patiently speaks to us from His Word after we've climbed out of a pit of self-pity.[22]

Remember, when you go deep into a cave, you eventually come to a dead end. It's difficult to look up. But when you step out of the cave, life is so much better.

He lifted me out of the pit of despair, out of the mud and the mire. He set my feet on solid ground and steadied me as I walked along. He has given me a new song to sing, a hymn of praise to our God.

—*Psalm 40:2–3* NLT

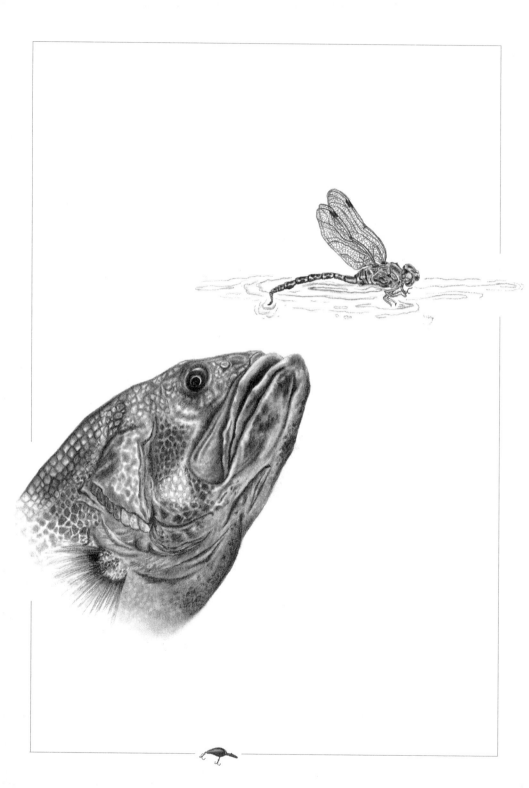

Strike Zone

31

In the spring of the year, America's national pastime—baseball—swings into high gear. This sport has its counterpart in bass fishing. It's the strike zone.

When the batter steps up to the plate, particular specifications need to be met for a pitch to be called a strike. Home plate is nineteen-and-a-half inches wide. The ball has to be thrown over it and at a certain height for the umpire to call a strike. Now, this zone can fluctuate in a couple of ways. The batter's height comes into play, and so does the perception of the umpire. Some umps are sticklers for the ball being right in that strike zone, while others really stretch it out, vertically and/or horizontally.

In the spring of 2001 umpires were ordered by major league baseball to follow the rule book definition of the strike zone that they'd been neglecting. The upper boundary is no longer at the belt line but is more around the armpit—literally "at the letters."[23]

If a pitcher wants to get strikeouts—or at least to avoid walking batters—he'd better hit that strike zone. He could have the right height but be a bit wide, or have the right width but be either too low or too high. If he can't throw strikes, he won't last long. He'll be replaced. Hitting the strike zone is a must in this sport.

It's a must in bass fishing as well. To be successful in bass fishing, it's not just a matter of finding bass. It's locating those that are willing to strike your offering at a particular time and place. It's discovering their strike window: the distance a bass will travel for food or to strike a lure. To add to the complexity, getting Mr. Bass to strike depends on several elements including the activity level of the fish, water clarity, and any obstacles that might be in the way.

Consider a bass's activity level. He's inactive, neutral, or active. This activity—or lack of it—determines the size of his strike zone (maybe there's some basis here for the variation we see in umpires). If a fish is inactive, he's got a very small window, or zone, right in front of his face. Your lure may need to be within a foot of his face and moving very slowly. So the less active the bass, the slower the presentation.

If he's in his neutral state, his strike window has expanded. He's not really on the prowl, but will go after something that looks vulnerable. And his attack is usually short and slow.

If the bass is active, watch out. He could come rushing out ten feet or more to attack. He swims faster and increases his forward range but loses some of his ability to turn to the side.

Let's complicate the strike window a bit more. If the water is clear, the strike window enlarges. Shade in shallow water has the same effect, but bright sunlight shrinks the window. Cold water tends to reduce it as well, whereas warm, stable weather expands it.

What does all this mean? Be sure you're hitting the strike zone. I've had days when I knew the bass were there, but I kept missing the zone. It could have been that my presentation or speed was off:

a small strike zone calls for a slow, more vertical presentation, while a large zone needs a rapid horizontal-moving presentation.[24]

Pitchers aren't the only ones to put forth effort and still miss the strike zone. And bass anglers aren't the only ones to make several hundred casts but still miss the strike zone. A husband could be diligent in demonstrating love to his spouse, but if it's not packaged in the right way or put in his wife's love language, he's missing his partner's strike zone.

Even in our Christian walk we could be missing the strike zone. We may be praying each day, but if we're not seeking God's will for our requests, we're missing it.

We could be committed to living life according to the Scriptures, but trying to do it ourselves instead of asking God for wisdom, guidance, or strength. Again, we're missing the strike zone.

Or we could have sat in church for years hearing message after message and yet never responded to the invitation to invite Jesus into our life as Lord and Savior. If this is the case, we've not only missed the strike zone, we're missing out on eternal life!

You are the salt of the earth. . . .
You are the light of the world.

—Matthew 5:13–14 NASB

Those Dreaded Words...

32

Certain words or phrases strike fear into the heart of even the strongest man. Take for instance those fateful words from his wife: "Dear, we need to talk." Those five words pack the emotional wallop of "code blue."

Well, there's a phrase in bass fishing that creates a similar response: *The bass are suspended.* For some this phrase creates nightmares, while it prompts others to throw in the towel and go home.

The language I heard from the boat a hundred feet away wasn't the best. This guy was really frustrated. He'd look at his graph, cast two or three times, look again, start casting, then look again. He did this for an hour. When I came closer, he said, "These stupid bass. I see scads of them, but they won't hit a top water, a bottom runner, or any plastic. What am I doing wrong?"

"Where are the bass located?" I asked.

He gave me a look like "Well, in the water, dummy. Where else?"

I said, "Where do you see them on your graph?" He turned the screen so I could see it. They weren't near the top or the bottom but right in the middle. "There's your problem. All those bass are suspended."

Now, why would an all-American, red-blooded fish do something like this to frustrate an angler?

First of all, because of a cold winter or a hot summer. These conditions slow down the bass's metabolism and they get sluggish. They also don't have a lot going on since it's not reproduction time. They'll move to a depth that has the most comfortable temperature and oxygen.

Other factors also can move bass into the suspended mode. Cold fronts or following a school of baitfish will pull them away from their usual haunts. If a lake or reservoir experiences a severe draw down, you've got instant suspension. Even too much boat traffic and fishing pressure can get them suspended.

Bass are difficult to catch at this time for several reasons. They're most likely in a dormant or sluggish state. They're in open water and not in their ambush posture; they like cover or structure for that. If they're hovering under a school of baitfish, just look at your competition. Why go after an imitation when you've got the real thing?

So what do you do? Give up and go home? Many anglers do. Others determine the depth of the fish and get their crankbait down, if possible, or fish vertically. I've watched an angler consistently bring in suspended bass one after another when no one else had a hook up. He uses a jig or doodles a worm. It can work. If suspended bass are a part of life, it's up to us to adapt to them, change our approach, and go catch 'em! It takes finesse, patience, and determination.[25]

I've seen suspended bass on my graph. They seemed to hang there immobile, vegetating, killing time. I've seen people just like them. They seem to simply exist. They take up space. Motivation is zero. They just hang out, and for some of them it's not only seasonal. This is their life. There are variations of this as well.

Some dads are phantomlike fathers, rarely involved with their sons or daughters.

Some merely exist within their marriages, never really participating or contributing.

Some are suspended in their Christian walk, sort of hanging in space, lethargic and immobile, not going anywhere.

It's kind of hard to be the *salt of the earth* or the *light of the world* as Jesus called us to be in His Sermon on the Mount when we're suspended.

Just as anglers would rather not see bass suspended, God would rather see us moving ahead, active, alive, and impacting the world for Him. I don't know about you, but I'd rather be on the move. True, it may be uncomfortable at times. That's all right. It's better to make waves than to simply tread water.

The fear of the Lord leads to life:
Then one rests content, untouched
by trouble.

—Proverbs 19:23

I'm Contented

33

*Y*ou've just eaten a huge meal at your favorite restaurant. Everything was seasoned and prepared the way you like it. You push back your chair, there's a smile on your face, and . . . you're content.

Contentment. It's an elusive dream for many. I've run into a number of discontented anglers. They're never satisfied. When you're never satisfied, you're not having much fun in life. You're constantly looking forward rather than getting the most out of the moment.

I overheard two bass anglers at the launch area one morning. Each one had a twenty-foot boat that looked as though it had been delivered new that morning. The colors of the boats and the trucks matched. Each boat was filled with the latest electronics and one of the largest live wells I'd ever seen. The walking space on the boats was second to none.

But the owners seemed to be saying the same thing. Each had owned his boat for less than a year but now was looking forward to the release of the new models so he could upgrade. I later learned they did this every year even though there was absolutely nothing wrong with what they had.

It's like a restless itch that we scratch, but the only relief is when we upgrade. I see the same itch when it comes to rods and reels. There's always something better out there.

I see it in relationships—this person doesn't satisfy anymore, so I'll look for someone else. That someone else may satisfy . . . and then again, may not.

Chariots of Fire, the fact-based, Oscar-winning movie, depicts the quest of Harold Abrahams and Eric Liddell to win gold medals in the 1924 Olympics, a feat they both accomplished. The difference between Abrahams and Liddell is transparent: Everything Abrahams did, he did for himself, while everything Liddell did was for the glory of God.

Eric's sister, Jennie, mistook her brother's love for running for rebellion against God and pressed him to return to the mission field in China, where they both were born and their parents lived. One day Jennie was upset because Eric had missed a mission meeting, so he decided to have a talk with her. They walked to a grassy spot overlooking the Scottish highlands.

Clutching her arms, trying to explain his calling to run, he said,

"Jennie, Jennie. You've got to understand. I believe God made me for a purpose—for China. But He also made me fast! And when I run, I feel His pleasure!"

That is in sharp contrast to a scene later in the movie, one hour before Harold Abrahams' final Olympic race. While his trainer gave him a rubdown, he lamented to his best friend, "I'm twenty-four and I've never known contentment. I'm forever in pursuit, and I don't even know what it is I'm chasing."

Each man won a gold medal, but one won his medal for himself, while the other won his medal for God. Do you feel God's pleasure in what you do, or, like Abrahams, does contentment elude you?

"I have learned the secret of being content in any and every situation" (Philippians 4:12).

If you haven't learned the secret, you can.

Too often we underestimate the power of a touch, a smile, a kind word, a listening ear.

Lunch With God

34

What do you share with other anglers when you're out on a lake? No, I don't mean what do you have in common—you're all fishing or using Shimano reels or sitting in a boat. Not that kind of share, but what do you give that's helpful and makes it easier for someone else?

What if you know the lake and its structure? Do you help someone who's never fished this lake before? If you've been nailing one bass after another, how do you answer someone who asks what you're using? What about the once-a-year dad who doesn't know squat about which end of the rod to hold and he's trying to teach his six-year-old son the joys of fishing? Do you go over and spend time getting them on the right track and leave them a few good lures? What about the guy who ran out of gas or his battery is dead? He should have planned ahead, but didn't. He needs some help, but it will cut into your fishing time. Or your buddy forgets his lunch, and you're starving?

So . . . what have you shared with others? A friend sent me an interesting story called *Lunch With God*:

A little boy wanted to meet God. He knew it was a long trip to where God lived, so he packed his suitcase with Twinkies and a six-pack of root beer and started his journey. When he had gone about three blocks, he met an old woman.

She was sitting in the park just staring at some pigeons. The boy sat down next to her and opened his suitcase. He was about to take a drink from his root beer when he noticed that the old lady looked hungry, so he offered her a Twinkie. She gratefully accepted it and smiled at him.

Her smile was so pretty that the boy wanted to see it again, so he offered her a root beer. Again, she smiled at him. The boy was delighted.

They sat there all afternoon eating and smiling, but they never said a word. As it grew dark, the boy realized how tired he was and he got up to leave, but before he had gone more than a few steps, he turned around, ran back to the old woman, and gave her a hug. She gave him her biggest smile ever.

When the boy opened the door to his house a short time later, his mother was surprised by the look of joy on his face. She asked him, "What did you do today that made you so happy?" He replied, "I had lunch with God." But before his mother could respond, he added, "You know what? She's got the most beautiful smile I've ever seen!"

Meanwhile, the old woman, also radiant with joy, returned to her home. Her son was stunned by the look of peace on her face, and he asked, "Mother, what did you do today that made you so happy?" She replied, "I ate Twinkies in the park with God." However, before her son responded, she added, "You know, He's much younger than I expected."

Too often we underestimate the power of a touch, a smile, a kind word, a listening ear, an honest compliment, or the smallest act of caring, all of which have the potential to turn a life around.

People come into our lives for a reason, a season, or a lifetime. Embrace all equally!

Have lunch with God.[26]

"I was hungry and you gave me food. I was thirsty and you gave me something to drink" (Matthew 25:35 NCV).

I was shown mercy . . . and the grace of our Lord was more than abundant, with the faith and love which are found in Christ Jesus.

—1 Timothy 1:13–14 *NASB*

The Tournament of Life

35

$\mathscr{Y}$ou enter an arena in Greensboro, North Carolina. Close to thirty thousand people are sitting in the stands waiting for the main event to begin. No, it's not a NASCAR race. It's the BASS Masters Classic weigh-in. Can you imagine that many people sitting there just to watch a bunch of bass being weighed? It's happening more and more. Bass fishing is becoming a major spectator sport, not only on TV but also at events. This is one of the few sports where people can get close to their heroes. Anglers come from as far away as Japan to participate.

Anyone can fish a tournament today. A tournament can be small and local or a national event. Your entry fee can vary from a few dollars to thousands. Local clubs hold tournaments and members can team up and compete.

But in a major money event you're matched with another

person. Your goal—bring back the largest five bass you can catch. Every ounce counts. You bring all your knowledge, ability, and skill to the forefront in a tournament.

Some pros follow a circuit 30 to 40 percent of the year. They live in motels, drive $70,000 to $100,000 rigs (vehicle and boat) across the country from one lake to another or one river to another. It's quite draining; a pro has to become proficient in many areas—not only an expert on lures, plastics, sizes, and colors, but maintenance of boat, trailer, and truck as well as lunar tables, weather, and water. And in addition, he or she has to develop something that's not as essential in other kinds of angling—a strong set of social skills. If you have sponsors, you're speaking, teaching, and connecting with people in their booths at the various shows. It's not an easy life.

Some tournaments really draw crowds. I'm not talking about fifty. I mean five thousand. That happened in 1996 at the KILT-FM 100 Bass Tournament in (where else?) Texas. Anyone could participate for an entry fee of $100. And it didn't matter what you fished out of. It could be a bass boat, rowboat, johnboat, or pontoon. Someone called it the angling equivalent to the Oklahoma land rush. And this tournament pays big-time. Every hour the tournament pays ten thousand dollars for the biggest fish, and you can win more than once. So if everything works perfectly, you could walk away with eighty thousand dollars—if you catch the biggest bass in each of the eight hours. (What are the odds of that?)

You've probably watched the really big tournaments where the top prize is from $70,000 to $100,000 or more. Wal-Mart's Forest Wood Open gives the largest—$200,000 to the top pro and $49,000 to the top amateur. Bass have really increased in value.[27]

At a BASSMASTER tournament in January 2001 at Lake Toho-pekaliga and the Kissimmee Chain in Florida, an Arizona pro, Dean Rojas, won $110,000 for first place. What was amazing was the total weight for his four-day limit—he broke the record. His opening day was 45 pounds 2 ounces, and his total was 108 pounds 12 ounces! This is one of those records that may never be broken. Talk about excitement.

Perhaps you've never fished in a bass tournament. Many haven't and never will. But every one of us is in another tourna-ment—the Tournament of Life. And no one has to be a loser. Every one of us can be a winner. We can all come out on top no matter how we've messed up in the past. All that's needed is to take a step of commitment to Jesus. That makes you a winner no matter what else happens. Trophies tarnish. This doesn't. Money drains away. The riches and blessings we have in our Christian life just keep growing.

It's a life worth exploring and experiencing. I hope you've dis-covered this already. We're called to press on in the Tournament of Life.

"If the work which any person has built on this Foundation—any product of his efforts whatever—survives (this test), he will get his reward" (1 Corinthians 3:14 AMP).

We press on and focus on the One who leads us.

> We have around us so many people whose lives tell us what faith means. So let us run the race that is before us and never give up. We should remove from our lives anything that would get in the way and the sin that so easily holds us back. Let us look only to Jesus, the One who began our faith and who makes it perfect. He suffered death on the cross. But he

accepted the shame as if it were nothing because of the joy that God put before him. And now he is sitting at the right side of God's throne. (Hebrews 12:1–2 NCV)

Invite others to join you to be winners in the Tournament of Life. They'll be glad you did. And so will you.

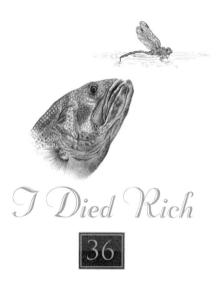

I Died Rich

36

*Y*ou've met them. So have I. They have tunnel vision and they're intense. They're what I call the obsessed bass angler. Their entire life is focused on getting to that lake and fishing. They think bass, talk bass, and everything else in life is secondary. Oh, sure, they have a job, a wife and kids, and go to PTA and church. But wherever they are, their minds are elsewhere. It's almost like an addiction. They can't let loose of it. Some fixate on their newest boat. They work on it, wax it, protect it, and wipe off every fingerprint several times a day. Others keep charts and graphs showing how the size of their largest bass creeps up and up and up. They dream of that twenty-two-and-a-half-pound world record.

I heard the story of two miners who spent half their lives looking for gold in the Pacific Northwest. Under the watchful eyes and criticism of the other people in town, the two miners pressed on, believing in their ability to strike it rich. These two became the joke of the town, as week after week they'd return from their mining with no gold. Nevertheless, they kept on with a deep confidence that someday they would find what they were looking for.

One hot afternoon, after months of digging in an old mine shaft, they finally hit pay dirt! Huge nuggets of gold were visible from a rich, previously undiscovered vein. Furiously, the men began pulling nugget after nugget from the earth.

No one knows whether it was a faulty support pole, the noise of shouting, or the gradual loosening of the dirt that caused the collapse, but the sound of loud, piercing cracks in the timber brought the two men to an abrupt halt. Suddenly the mineshaft caved in, and an avalanche of dirt pounded both men to the floor.

One of the men lay injured on the ground, grasping a large nugget he'd found. The other miner, still able to move, pulled himself up and yelled, "Come on! We've got to get out of here before the whole thing collapses! I'll help you! Get up! Leave the gold. We don't have a second to lose!"

The injured miner, still holding the gold nugget, said, "No. Just leave me here. I found what I've been looking for. I've spent my life searching for this vein, and I'm not about to let it go now. Leave me here. You go! Get out of here."

"Don't be foolish! We've gotta get you out!" his partner replied. Just then, the rafters trembled again, spilling more dirt into the dust-filled shaft. "If I leave you here, you'll die! What'll I tell your family?! What'll I tell the folks back in town?"

The badly injured miner wheezed his final words between strained coughs as dust filled the collapsing chamber. "Just tell 'em

I died rich," he whispered with a final breath. "Just tell 'em I died rich."[28]

Whether it's a gold nugget, a new bass boat, or a life consumed by always being out there chasing the bass, it's the same problem—priorities out of balance.

Didn't Jesus say something about this?

Do not gather and heap up and store for yourselves treasures on earth, where moth and rust and worm consume and destroy, and where thieves break through and steal; But gather and heap up and store for yourselves treasures in heaven, where neither moth nor rust nor worm consume and destroy, and where thieves do not break through and steal; For where your treasure is, there will your heart be also. . . . No one can serve two masters; for either he will hate the one and love the other, or he will stand by and be devoted to the one and despise and be against the other. You cannot serve God and mammon [that is, deceitful riches, money, possessions, or what is trusted in]. (Matthew 6:19–21, 24 AMP)

Listen to your heart. It will tell you whether or not you're on course.

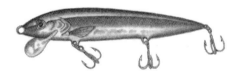

*L*isten to advice and accept
correction, and in the end you will
be wise.

—*Proverbs 19:20* NCV

The Ten-Pounder

37

What's your bass fishing dream? If you're like most it's landing that ten-pounder. Many anglers spend their entire life chasing that dream. They go from state to state, lake to lake, guide to guide, hoping one day to connect with that magical weight. Some people fish for thirty to forty years, yet this fish eludes them. I know guides who have yet to connect.

What's a ten-pound bass like? Why is he so difficult to catch? Oops. There's the first misbelief—he. It's not usually the male that you catch. Fishery experts tell us that a male rarely gets above six pounds. It's the female . . . and she *is* big! You could double both fists and put them in her mouth.

How does she get that large? By being smart. It's as simple as that. She's cautious, free of disease, and healthy. She's solitary, more territorial than others. When it comes to food she's not so aggressive in pursuing, but is more cautious and discriminating. Often this fish lives in an area that's difficult for an angler to approach. She's wise in knowing the difference between live and artificial. And some studies show she suspends feeding during the day and gets active at night.

One of the best-known pros is Shaw Grigsby. In one year he landed ten bass over ten pounds and all in the same lake. In his book *Bass Master Shaw Grigsby*, he talks about another angler, Doug Hannon, who has caught more than five hundred bass over ten pounds. Can you even imagine such a feat? It was interesting to hear what he said about catching them. Almost all were caught in shallow water and most between 10:00 A.M. and 3:00 P.M.[29]

During the first two years of the Lunker Club (catches over ten pounds) for *Bassmaster* magazine, 278 catches were submitted. March and April led the months when the most were caught, followed by January and February. Almost 40 percent hit in water between sixty and seventy degrees. Plastic worms, live shiners, jig-and-pig, and spinnerbaits were the top four lures or baits. Florida (26.6 percent), Texas (18.7 percent), and California (16.2 percent) led the states in catches. Naturally, Lake Fork in Texas led the list for the most lunker catches during this time (thirty-two).

What's your largest bass so far? What's your dream? Like most, I wanted to catch that lunker. But not really getting into bass fishing until I was in my late fifties, I wondered about the possibility. In the spring of 2000, I went on a couple of outings with a well-known California guide, Bob Crupi. On my first trip with him to Castaic Lake I hit a nine-pound, two-ounce beauty. I was delighted. That was my big fish for my lifetime. But the next month I landed a ten-pound, one-ounce bass. It was hard to believe. During her first rush we didn't think she was that large. But then she came out from under a buoy line, under the boat and an anchor rope. All I could think was keep the pressure on, reel when she stops, and don't let the eight-pound line hit the bottom of the boat. And then we scooped her into the net—it was a thrill. (That was the same day I caught a seven- and two five-pounders!)

How did this happen? It wasn't due to my knowledge and skill, that's for sure. I listened to Bob, following his directions to the letter. And it took patience.

It's easy to miss out on opportunities because we don't follow those life principles. Impatient decisions and acts not only cause people to miss out on something they want but can also lead to results they regret the rest of their lives.

Even a little thing such as impatience in what you say has far-reaching results: "Do you see a man who speaks in haste? There is more hope for a fool than for him" (Proverbs 29:20)—one translation puts it "blurts out." What's your degree of patience in what you say?

How are you about being taught? Are you a good student? There's a benefit, as Proverbs states:

> The mind of a person with understanding gets knowledge;
> the wise person listens to learn more. (Proverbs 18:15 NCV)
> A wise warning to someone who will listen is as valuable as
> gold earrings or fine gold jewelry. (Proverbs 25:12 NCV)

How would your family members describe your openness to instruction?

Shaw Grigsby has some final instructions on catching ten-pounders. To catch them, you have to do everything right. And even if you do, it could be years before you hook one. If you hook one.[30]

Hmm—there's still some uncertainty, isn't there? Well, there's one fact that is certain, that we can all rely on. God loves us. And that's better than a ten-pounder any day.

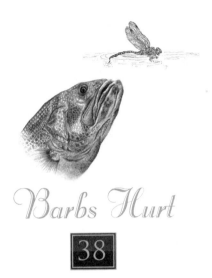

Barbs Hurt

38

*Y*ou've got to be careful with hooks. I know. When that sharp hook invades your skin and sinks into your flesh deep enough so the barb gains a grip, you're in for some pain. The more you pull, the more the barb grabs and holds on.

I've seen hooks and lures hanging from a hand, an arm, and—one time—dangling from an ear like some newly fashioned earring. But it wasn't a pretty sight.

Who hasn't put his hand into his fishing kit or satchel and yelped upon finding a loose hook?

On my first Canadian pike fishing adventure, we caught northerns until our arms ached. We must have made hundreds of casts. And each time we did, we swung that daredevil lure behind us and whipped over the water to land inches from shore. One time, though, it went flying out attached to the hat of our guide. I don't know who was more shocked, my partner, who is three-quarters Cherokee, or our guide, a full-blooded Native American. He'd said just four or five words up to this time, but now he looked at my partner with a deadpan expression and said, "Huh. This first time one Indian scalp another Indian," and then burst out laughing. Fortunately that experience worked out all right—but not so with the next one.

A guide shared this one with me: Several bass guides were waiting inside a restaurant at a marina for their clients to show. Suddenly an intense, portly guy burst through the door, "All right, where's my guide? I'm ready to go. I'm paying good money for this. Time's a wasting. Let's get this show on the road!" He continued to mumble and grumble, stomping around the restaurant. The four guides in the back room went silent, hoping he wouldn't find them, and more than that, hoping and praying this guy wasn't *their* client.

In a few minutes another guide came in, talked to the man, went to the back room, and said, "Relax, guys—you're off the hook. I'm the doomed one today."

So he rounded up the loud, pushy angler, took off, and started fishing. As they went to change location, the guide asked him to attach the lure to the rod, strap it down, and take a seat. The man didn't comply and said he'd hold on to it. They took off, and as they gained speed it became bumpier. With each bump and sway of the boat the angler let out a grunt or swore or yelped. All of a sudden there wasn't a sound. The guide glanced over. The man's eyes were huge; his mouth was open but no sound was coming out. The guide brought the boat to a halt. As he did the man slowly got up, legs bowed, still holding the rod. He pointed with one hand

and then the guide saw it. His eyes followed the line coming from the tip down to the lure. Now, the lure was good sized with number two hooks. But one of those hooks was embedded (and I mean embedded) in a, well, an unmentionable place in the guy's groin. He'd hooked himself right *there*—yes, you know what I mean!

Just imagine you're the guide—think of what you should say (or shouldn't or would want to).

What would you do? Talk about wanting to help someone in agony and on the other hand not wanting to touch him with a ten-foot pole! Imagine the ride back to the dock, each bump and sway of the boat. Think of the first thought you'd have if you were the nurse or doctor at the ER when this bow-legged guy shuffles through the door with a dangling lure and pain all over his face! (Let's not go there.) Worse yet, the guide had to put up with all the wise cracks from the other guides for weeks!

Hooks hurt. Barbs hurt, and barbs on hooks aren't the only ones that can wound. There are other ways to be wounded or to wound others. Words are one of the surest ways to sink a painful barb into a person, and Job knew this. He listened to his friends endlessly hammer at him. Finally, he'd had it and said, "How long will you vex and torment me, and break me in pieces with words?" (Job 19:2 AMP).

Proverbs tells us:

> With his mouth the godless man destroys his neighbor. (Proverbs 11:9 AMP)
> Careless words stab like a sword, but wise words bring healing. (Proverbs 12:18 NCV)
> Pleasant words are like a honeycomb, making people happy and healthy. (Proverbs 16:24 NCV)

Death and life are in the power of the tongue, and they who indulge it shall eat the fruit of it [for death or life]. (Proverbs 18:21 AMP)

Barbs have their place on hooks but not on our words. A hooked bass is released and goes on his way none the worse for wear. But a person who's been hooked with a word carries the wounds of the barb, sometimes for years.

Superstitious Anglers

39

"Me? Superstitious? Naw! Not me." Are you? Fishermen seem to have a unique set of superstitious behaviors. And some are dead serious about them. Have you ever said something like "Hey! This is my lucky hat. I wouldn't make a cast without it" or "I *always* make my first three casts with this lure. It's the only way to start the day. You can't believe the number of bass I've caught with it."

As a bass guide and I skimmed across the water, he made a quick turn, and a small green container went flying out of the boat. The guide saw it, said, "Oh no!" and did a hard 180-degree turn to get to where the container was slowly filling with water. He scooped it up just before it sank and said, "This is my special urinal can. It's been with me forever. I can't lose this." Oh well.

One day I read an article by a local newspaper writer, Jed Welsh. He talked about a couple of superstitious behaviors. One I'd heard before: Spit on your bait or lure for good luck. Some anglers won't make a cast unless they've spit. Jed said that he's spit on every lure, bait, or fly that he's ever cast. Sure, a lot of people talk about him and his odd custom of spitting and fishing, but one of America's noted fishing authorities on fly-fishing, Professor Michaels of Cal Tech, said, "Spitting on bait is not really an old wives' tale as so many think. Human saliva contains a solution called pectin, which is essential for the digestive process. The odor of this can attract a feeding bird, animal, or a fish." So there is a purpose for this so-called superstition.

But here's one that's really far out: Never take bananas on a fishing boat. Now, those who fish salt water seem to know all about this superstition, and what's surprising, they even practice it. In fact, sometimes a boat's crewmember will go through everyone's lunches and throw all the bananas overboard. He doesn't want the fishing expedition to be jinxed. Can you imagine this? When I heard it, I wondered if they peeled them first or mashed them or . . .

Jed Welsh had just the opposite experience. He was ocean fishing off Costa Rica, and the local skipper peeled a half-green, half-yellow banana and sliced the skin three-fourths of the way in quarter-inch strips. He put a large hook through the end and began to troll. The banana strips fluttered and wiggled and the lure splashed and jumped out of the water. By the end of the day two sailfish and two dorado were landed on that superstition-breaking lure.

What about you? Are any little idiosyncrasies or quirks part of your fishing life? A superstition is really nothing more than something we've learned to depend on or trust in. Some build their entire life on little rituals like these. Some build their lives trusting mainly in themselves. There are some who trust in something else, though. They've learned to trust in the Lord.

There's a difference between living life based on superstition and living it on trust. Superstition is a belief based on fear or ignorance. That's inconsistent with what is really true.

Trust, on the other hand, is to hope, believe, have an expectation with a high degree of confidence. It's true, you can trust in the wrong thing. I've heard advice from some bass anglers I wouldn't trust. But I value the word of others. If I'm going to trust, I want it to be in something that's certain. I don't want it to be a superstitious myth. I've found something to really trust in. The writer of Proverbs said it well: "Trust the Lord with all your heart, and don't depend on your own understanding. Remember the Lord in all you do, and he will give you success" (Proverbs 3:5–6 NCV).

So . . . in whom do you trust? There's One we can always count on.

𝓑e imitators of God, therefore, as dearly loved children and live a life of love, just as Christ loved us and gave himself up for us.

—Ephesians 5:1–2

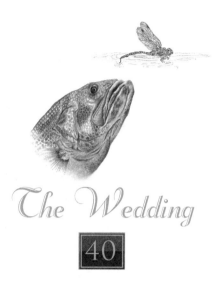

The Wedding

40

The mail arrives. You sort through it and see an envelope with a familiar look—it appears for all the world to be a wedding invitation. But upon opening it, you're looking at the most unusual invitation you've ever seen. It's an application to a bass tournament. That's right, a bass tournament. But it's *also* a wedding invitation!

It was probably the strangest invitation and wedding anyone will ever see. It took place on Fork Lake in Texas. It was even written up in the book *Fly-Fishing for Sharks*. Everyone was invited to fish in the tournament. And why not? The groom was one of the Fork Lake guides, and the bride could hold her own with bass as well.

Instead of sending in an RSVP card to let them know you'd be there, you just mailed in your application, bought a wedding gift, went over your equipment to get it ready for the tournament, and waited for the big day.

When the day came you went out to a marina at the lake for the festivities and launched your boat. These were not your average church pews. People were on docks and in boats. The groom was there waiting for the bride. You know how everyone waits for the processional and the bride and her father to come down the aisle? Well, this too was a bit different. The father accompanied the bride to the altar, but your first glimpse of them was a speck about a half-mile away. You may have heard them before you saw them. Streaking across the surface of Fork Lake was a bass boat with the father of the bride at the wheel, the bride sitting next to him with a forty-foot veil trailing behind the boat. When they neared the dock, the bride's dad made a sharp turn, creating a wave, and the veil wrapped itself around the bride's head! The attendees thought it was great. (It was a fairly raucous group.) Once the bride and groom completed their vows, the groom's brother came running up and threw the groom into the lake. Now they could get to the real business of the day—the tournament.

You'll see and hear about some strange happenings with bass anglers.

A lot of strange things happen at "regular" weddings too, especially when they're in a location other than a church.

One setting that lends itself to the possibility of uncontrollable, unanticipated disastrous events is the outdoor wedding. The first one I helped officiate was in the backyard of a private home in a nice neighborhood. We weren't more than two minutes into the service before we had to stop. A small plane that had just taken off from a nearby airport was drowning out even the loudest speaker. Finally it departed and we were moving further into the service when a commercial jet took off, not only drowning us out but shaking the ground as well. Everyone by this time began to look at one another and laugh. Finally we could hear again, but within a few minutes an enormous flock of blackbirds flew into one of the trees and proceeded to chatter. I'm not sure which was worse—the birds or the planes!

By this time it was late morning in early summer in Southern California. You guessed it. The temperature was rising! It was getting warm—quite warm—and the other officiating minister and I were in suits. I hoped the sweat wasn't too obvious as it began to trickle down our foreheads.

The payoff, though, was the dog. Not an ordinary dog, but one of those dorky, prissy types. It looked like a small, detached mop. It ambled out and headed for—you guessed it—the two of us conducting the service and the bride and groom. The dog stood between us, first looking at the bride and groom and then at my friend and me. Now, you've got to understand the dynamics here. My friend Rex and I have worked together for years teaching and conducting seminars. We know how the other thinks, and we kid and joke around a lot. With the dog looking back and forth, I knew what Rex was thinking and he knew what I was thinking: "Is that dog going to hike his leg or not?" I didn't dare look at Rex or we both would have doubled over with laughter, since this dog was the last straw. And the look on the bride and groom's faces confirmed that a similar thought had crossed their minds.

What do you remember about your wedding? What stands out in your memory? What do you remember about your courtship? When was the last time you and your spouse reflected on your marital journey? This could be an enlightening discussion.

Perhaps the most important question about your marriage is this: In what way do you see your relationship with Jesus affecting the way you respond to your spouse? One of the best (and hardest) places to live out your faith in life is in your marriage. It's certainly worth considering. And while you're doing that just remember, the first miracle that Jesus performed was at a wedding. He's still performing miracles in marriages today.

*What do you remember about
your wedding? What do you
remember about your courtship?*

Older Is Better

41

You caught a two-pound bass in Oklahoma; how old was it?

You caught a two-pound bass in the Mississippi River between Iowa and Illinois. How old was *that* one? You'd probably say, *"Come on, they're both the same."* Not necessarily. The Mississippi is a muddy river, and a bass living there could take five years to reach twelve inches. The Okie fish, on the other hand, grows much faster. It has clearer water and a longer growing season. There's a lot of variation, since there are many factors involved.

But who wants to know about a two-pounder? We all want those trophy bass. How old are they? Do you recall how to tell the age of a pine tree? You count the annual rings.

And remember, only a few bass live longer than ten years. The few that do are probably in the record book.

Let's get back to those rings. You can accurately figure out a bass's age by counting the growth rings from almost any bony structure of its body, according to fish biologists. When a fish grows, new bony structure is added in circular fashion like the rings of growth you see on trees. And whereas mammals reach their size in two or three years, bass just keep on growing.

Where do you look? At their scales. By measuring the distance between these rings and knowing the length of the fish, a fish biologist can calculate the length of any fish at a given age.[31]

It's one thing to note the length and weight of that trophy bass, but the next time you catch one, see if you can determine its age. The bass won't mind. He's not sensitive about it like we are. We seem to have this hang-up about getting older and letting others know our "real" age. Aging is just part of life. How old are you? No, we're not going to count the rings on your skin or gray hairs on your head.

In the Bible, getting older and being older is counted as a blessing. It's a time of honor. Sure, there are lots of changes that we don't particularly care for. Solomon described these:

> Remember your Creator in the days of your youth, before the days of trouble come and the years approach when you will say, "I find no pleasure in them"—before the sun and the light and the moon and the stars grow dark, and the clouds return after the rain; when the keepers of the house tremble, and the strong men stoop, when the grinders cease because they are few, and those looking through the windows grow dim; when the doors to the street are closed and the sound of grinding fades; when men rise up at the sound of birds, but all their songs grow faint; when men are afraid of heights and of dangers in the streets; when the almond tree blossoms and the grasshopper drags himself along and desire no longer is stirred. Then man goes to his eternal home and mourners go about the streets. (Ecclesiastes 12:1–5)

That's fairly blunt. Aging is a fact of life. We think a lot about it. Bass don't. Perhaps they're the fortunate ones.

The psalmist gave us excellent advice when he said, "Teach us to number our days aright, that we may gain a heart of wisdom" (Psalm 90:12).

Moses was credited with writing this psalm. What did he do for years? He was a shepherd. He counted sheep so that none ended up missing. And unless he counts, and counts well, he can't be sure all of them are there. We too need to number our days in this brief life to make sure none end up missing—that we don't squander a day, since every one is a gift from God. Don't let any day slip by. Use each one. Embrace each one. Look for God in each one. Enjoy each one. Begin each day by thanking God for the day and saying, "How can I use this day for you, Lord?"

Spend your time and energy in training yourself for spiritual fitness. Physical exercise has some value, but spiritual exercise is much more important, for it promises a reward in both this life and the next.

—1 Timothy 4:7–8 NLT

There Are No Shortcuts

For some people, shortcuts are part of life. If they can save time or energy by eliminating some steps in a process, they'll do it. We're encouraged to take shortcuts. Listen to all the get-rich-quick schemes we hear about. Why do we get hooked into those "lose thirty pounds in thirty days" diet schemes? Would we bite if the offer were "lose thirty pounds in ninety days"? Not likely. What about "learn to speak a foreign language fluently in just sixteen easy at-home audio lessons—nothing to read!" Why take two years of college classes when you can do it in one-tenth of the time?

Perhaps you've taken a shortcut while hiking or driving only to discover it took you twice as long to get there. That's the problem with many shortcuts. They don't work. They're often longer in the end, or you bypass or leave out some essentials. Even though you got there, or finished much sooner, you weren't well equipped.

I've gotten lost on fishing trips. Perhaps you've done the same. Perhaps you got directions to a new fishing area. You looked at a map and decided it would be quicker and shorter to take a different route. Two hours later you're stuck at the edge of a logging road with no place to turn your van and boat around.

A friend and I decided to hike to a High Sierra lake. We'd been there before, but decided after looking at a topographical map to cut across country to make it easier. But these maps don't show the lack of trails, deadfalls to climb through, and small cliffs to scale. We started out and an hour later had no idea where we were, and I had fallen over a log and developed a choice-looking bruise. We kept on going up a hill from which we surely would see the lake or the trail. Not so. We only saw the other side of the hill with all its cliffs and ledges. Two hours later we decided to retreat. Fortunately we found the edge of another lake and flagged down a passing boat to beg a ride.

Shortcuts don't work in catching bass, either. I've seen anglers in a boat cut through an area of a lake where other anglers were working on fish instead of slowing down and going around.

I've seen *many* anglers who did not take the time to read articles or books or watch videos about how to catch fish. Rather, they come up to you and want to get all the latest info in five minutes that you've spent dozens of hours collecting, so they can get out there and catch fish.

I don't know many pros who would take a shortcut by skipping the days of pre-fishing a tournament. In all areas of life we have to pay the dues and put in the time and effort it takes to make things work. And this includes our faith.

Scripture illustrates the fact that to attain you have to train.

There are no shortcuts to Christian growth. It takes training, and this means work, diligence, sweat, persistence, and practice. Paul said, "Everyone who competes in the games goes into strict training. They do it to get a crown that will not last; but we do it to get a crown that will last forever" (1 Corinthians 9:25).

Now let's meddle a bit. Are you married?

It's the same way in marriage. There are no shortcuts to having a fulfilling, rewarding marriage. You have to put in the hours of conversation, of consistently being attentive and sensitive in order to build closeness. It won't happen overnight. And you can't read "thirty days to super sex and super marriage" as a substitute for diligence.

So when tempted to cut corners in giving time and attention to any area of life . . . don't. It's a good way to get lost on the lake, in the mountains, in your marriage . . . or in any area of life.

*The free gift of God is eternal life
in Christ Jesus our Lord.*

—Romans 6:23 NASB

The Gift

43

I was given a gift at church one day. A woman asked me to sign my first bass devotional, *The Perfect Catch*, for her family and then gave me two books from her husband's bass book collection. When I saw them, I was excited. One was a collection of articles, *The Best of Bassmaster*. The other was *Book of the Black Bass—Scientific and Life History, Together With a Practical Treatise on Angling and Fly-Fishing and a Full Description of Tools, Tackle, and Implements*, by James A. Henshall, M.D. How's that for a title? It is a reprint of a book that was first published in 1881! What a find. This 463-page book includes the original drawings, sketches, and illustrations.

What an angling treasure! Do you know what this author said about bass more than one hundred twenty years ago? He described a bass as the perfect fish: "Inch for inch and pound for pound the gamest fish that swims." He looked into the future when he said,

"The Black Bass is wholly unknown in the Old World except where recently introduced, and exists, naturally, only in America. . . . No doubt the Black Bass is the appointed successor to the Lordly Trout. . . . He will eventually become the leading game fish of America is my oft-expressed opinion and firm belief" (iii). He was so right.

It's fascinating to read this book not only to learn what was believed about bass years ago but also to see the writing style. The author tracked down the first description of a bass to 1800 by a Frenchman who was sent a distorted specimen from this country. Dr. Henshall gave this description: "This representation of American fish was first brought to the light of science in a foreign land and under the most unfavorable auspices. Its scientific birth was untimely; it was unhappily born a monstrosity; its baptismal names were, consequently, incongruous, and its sponsors were most unfortunately foreign naturalists."[32] The author traces all of the references to the black bass from 1800 through 1878 with the various Latin names and descriptions.

Perhaps you assume, like many, that bass were everywhere. Not so. They were carefully carried and restocked from lake to lake. The author gave specific accounts of how "Mr. So-and-So" brought twenty-seven bass from one lake to another lake. In 1851 and 1852 two hundred bass had been stocked in ponds near East Wareham, Massachusetts. He stated, "The matter was kept quiet and fishing discouraged for five years, when the fish were found to have increased very rapidly."[33] Remember, back then it wasn't catch and release. It was catch and eat!

I don't know how you would have liked to fish with the rods of the last century, but here are some specs on them. They ranged in length from eleven to twenty feet. The various woods included (sorry, no graphite) cane, ash, hickory, maple, basswood, ironwood, hornbeam, cedar, barberry, bamboo, memel, lancewood, mahoe, greenheart, bethabarce. The author evaluated each one, which I'll spare you.

Rods for bass were shortened to eight feet, two-piece, with an adjustable handle.

The *Book of the Black Bass* was a refreshing change with its historical perspective. We certainly have come a long way in our pursuit of bass.

This book has become very special to me, a gift from the library of Wayne Garber. I've never met him, only his wife who gave me these two books. I do have a picture of him holding a nice-sized bass at a lake. On the back of the picture he wrote, "Lake Casitas—the place where you can listen and see God." He said he never felt closer to God than when he was out on the lake.

Wayne received a gift, too. It was free with no strings attached. He received it, but it wasn't fully experienced at that moment. It came as part of the promise of accepting Jesus as His Savior in 1984. That in itself was a blessing for his daily life; the other part was the promise of eternal life. Wayne is experiencing that now. In July 2000 he entered into the presence of Jesus. He's met Him face-to-face. And it's great to know that he doesn't miss bass fishing at all. Someday I'll get to see both Wayne and Jesus face-to-face. I hope you will too.

*But Jesus immediately said to
them: "Take courage! It is I. Don't
be afraid."*

—*Matthew 14:27*

You've Got to Get Out of the Boat!

44

You've heard it. You've probably said it. "Stay in the boat." It's good advice, especially when the alternative is getting wet. Most of us have both humorous and embarrassing stories of someone or something that didn't stay in the boat. I've seen a family member start to get out of the boat too soon. One leg was still in the boat and one on the edge of the dock. So as he pushed with his foot on the dock instead of the one in the boat, the inevitable happened. The gap between the boat and the dock widened. So did the stretch of this man. He and everyone watching knew what was about to happen. And it did. He got soaked.

I have a friend who takes his Lab, Buck, with him when he goes fishing for bass and crappie. Many, many times he has told Buck, "Stay in the boat." But if he uses a bobber and bait, as soon as Buck sees that bobber flying through the air, he thinks, *retrieve*, and he does. There goes fishing for the day.

What have you lost out of a boat? Think about it. Most of us have given up something to the depths of a river or a lake. The other day I thought of all the different items I wished had stayed in the boat but didn't. I couldn't believe the wide variety. They ranged from a dog to a knife, pliers, lure, a fishing partner (who still can't figure out how he fell in), glasses, a Loomis rod with a Shimano reel (I don't want to talk about that experience), the drain plug for the boat, and the last piece of moist, mocha-flavored, killer chocolate cake (I almost cried over that one).

All in all, it's better to stay in the boat. In fact, that's what some people feel Peter should have done when he saw Jesus walking on the water. Remember the story?

> During the fourth watch of the night Jesus went out to them, walking on the lake. When the disciples saw him walking on the lake, they were terrified. "It's a ghost," they said, and cried in fear.
>
> But Jesus immediately said to them: "Take courage! It is I. Don't be afraid."
>
> "Lord, if it's you," Peter replied, "tell me to come to you on the water."
>
> "Come," he said.
>
> Then Peter got down out of the boat, walked on the water and came toward Jesus. But when he saw the wind, he was afraid and, beginning to sink, cried out, "Lord, save me!"
>
> Immediately Jesus reached out his hand and caught him.

"You of little faith," he said, "why did you doubt?" (Matthew 14:25–32).

When Peter said, "Lord, if it's you, tell me to come to you on the water," Jesus invited him to do so. Was Peter scared? Probably. I would be. I've been in storms before. Those waves have the word *drown* written all over them. But if Peter wanted to walk on the water, he had to run the risk of getting out of the boat. At least he was willing to do that. There are many who would look at that wild wind and say, "Not on your life." At first, all Peter really saw or focused on was Jesus. And he walked. Then he took his eyes off Jesus and focused on the wind. And he sank.

I'm a lot like Peter. Perhaps you are, too. Perhaps we all are. We're hesitant to take a risk. Maybe we think Jesus is calling us to follow Him in some area of our life, but all we can feel is the wind. You know, obstacles. We want to follow Him but there's a lot of uncertainty. *"If only I could be risk-free and certain, I'd follow"* is what a lot of us think. Staying in the boat of life is comfortable. John Ortberg wrote the book *If You Want to Walk on Water, You've Got to Get Out of the Boat.* Consider a few of his thoughts. They may prompt you to try water-walking.

> The call to get out of the boat involves crisis, opportunity, often failure, generally fear, sometimes suffering, always the calling to a task too big for us. But there is no other way to grow faith and to partner with God.
>
> So, where are you in relation to Jesus these days?
> Huddled in the boat with a life preserver and seat belt on,
> One leg in, one leg out,

I'm walking on the water—and loving it.
I'm out of the boat—the wind looks pretty bad.[34]

Jesus is still looking for people who will get out of the boat. I don't know what this means for you. If you get out of your boat—whatever your boat happens to be—you will have problems. There is a storm out there, and your faith will not be perfect. Risk always holds the possibility of failure.

But if you get out, I believe two things will happen. The first is that when you fail—and you will fail sometimes—Jesus will be there to pick you up. You will not fail alone. You will find that He is still wholly adequate to save.

And the other thing is, every once in a while you will walk on water.

Who's in Charge of Your Time?

45

"I'd just like to pass the time away."

"I can't afford to waste my time."

"Soon my time restraints will be lifted, and I will . . ."

"I'm going to find the time this year to . . ."

"Someday, when I get time, I'm going to . . ."

These are common phrases. Well-intentioned phrases. Phrases meant to correct, simplify, streamline. Phrases designed to ease tension and to give us hope. But they're phrases that all too often remain empty dreams.

How do you "get time" or "find time" or "restrain time" or "waste time"? Think about some of the words that describe how we use our time. We stretch it. (I didn't know time was elastic!) We juggle it. (Does time come in balls, hoops, or pins?) And we schedule it. (Do we use a timer for time?)

In fact, how do you even define the word *time*? How do you explain it? Did you ever stop to wonder whether Adam and Eve had a sense of time? Did they have some sort of clock to mark the passing of the hours? Probably not.

The first clocks were introduced during the 1200s and were some kind of alarm. In the 1300s the dial and hour hand were added. By the 1600s the minute and second hands were in evidence.[35] Look at some gift catalogs today, or go into a department store. You'll be amazed at the variation and sophistication of the "time-saving" timepieces available today.

Just as clocks have been around for centuries, so has frustration with time constraints. People complained about the sundial in 200 B.C.! Plautus wrote, "The gods confound the man who first found out how to distinguish hours! Confound him, too, who in this place set up a sundial to cut and hack my days so wretchedly into small portions."[36]

Well, one thing about bass anglers—we know how they use their time and that most of them wish they had *more* time to fish. By the way, just how many days a year do *you* fish? Ever kept track? And on the days you fish, how much time do you spend fishing? There's a reason for my asking (and it's all right to spend time pursuing bass).

Anglers differ in the amount of time they spend fishing. Perhaps you can use the following information to convince others that you need to spend more time with a rod in your hands.

Were you aware that each year in the United States thirty-five million anglers over the age of sixteen fish for a total of 626 million days? And there are three types of anglers. Those who fish one or two years out of five are called "infrequent" anglers. They probably didn't fish as children and are likely to be women and members of minority groups. "Sporadic" anglers are those who fish three or four years out of five and are apt to be female and sixty-five years or older. Then we have the "avid" anglers who fish every year. They make up sixty-five percent of anglers and are apt to be white males.

Which category do you fit into? And how many days a year do you fish? If it's one to nine days, you're right in there with 51 percent of anglers. What if you fish thirty to ninety-nine days or (better yet) 100 to 350 days? The latter group makes up only 2 percent of anglers, whereas those who fish thirty to ninety-nine days make up 15 percent.[37] Which group would you like to be in?

Some would give their eyeteeth to be able to fish four or five days a year. Perhaps we ought to be thankful for any time we have to fish, especially when we really don't have that many days to do as we would like.

Years ago someone wrote an article with this attention-getting title: "If You Are 35, You Have 500 Days to Live." Your first reaction might be, "Wait a minute, that couldn't be true!" Consider what the author says, though. When you take away all the time spent sleeping, working, doing chores, taking care of personal hygiene, attending to personal matters, eating, and traveling, you end up with only five hundred days in the next thirty-six years to spend as you want. Isn't that sobering? It sheds new light on the psalmist's words: "Teach us to make the most of our time, so that we may grow in wisdom" (Psalm 90:12 NLT).

How are you using the time God has given you? Do you look back at the end of the day and say, "God gave me twenty-four hours today. I did put it to good use for Him, others, and myself." If so, you're on target. If not, perhaps a time-use correction is in order.

God wants us to be wise in the use of our time for a good reason.

"See then that you walk circumspectly, not as fools but as wise, redeeming the time, because the days are evil" (Ephesians 5:15–16 NKJV).

What Are You Accomplishing?

46

*W*hat are your major bass fishing accomplishments? Is it the number of bass you've caught in one day? I know some anglers who have caught seventy or eighty in a day. Is it the size of your fish? Most of us want to catch that double-digit bass. Some do, but many don't. I fished with one professional guide who'd been at it for twenty-five years. His largest was eight pounds. I've fished with another guide who's the only angler to catch two bass over twenty—that's right, twenty pounds.

Some live for their accomplishments. If they don't catch more or bigger fish each time they go out, they're bummed for the rest of the week. Not only do they set themselves up for an impossible task, they're missing the enjoyment of just getting out there on the water! There are some who expect to do better each time without putting forth the effort of reading, watching, listening, and practicing. They too are going to be disappointed.

How much are accomplishments a part of your life?

Most of us like to be able to list a few. Even when we were kids we liked to have ribbons, trophies, or awards to show. But to accomplish something, you've got to stick with it, even against the pain and the odds.

How does the guy who started out as a dishwasher at seventeen, right out of high school, get to be CEO of that same restaurant chain at thirty-five? By hard work. He didn't give up. He attracted attention because of his attention.

To be an accomplished angler, or to be proficient in any area, you have to do whatever the task is or learn the skill completely. You don't leave loose ends. You don't complete it to a 97 percent level and never get back to what's left. You're thorough. Webster defines accomplishment this way: "Done through to the end, complete, omitting nothing; accurate; very exact."[38]

When you do something in this way it will reflect a pattern of excellence.

Pastor Joe Brown, a former Navy officer, shared this story about giving our best effort to everything we do.

As a young man, Jimmy Carter graduated from the Naval Academy and served as an officer on a nuclear-powered submarine. However, before he was able to assume that position, he had to have a personal interview with Admiral Hyman Rickover, the man considered to be the father of the nuclear navy. Carter was understandably nervous, knowing how much was at stake and that only the best, most disciplined officers were chosen to serve in this prestigious force.

When he stood before Rickover, it was soon obvious to the young officer that the wise officer knew more about nearly every subject discussed than did he. Finally Rickover came to the last question on his seemingly never-ending list. "Where did you finish in your class, young man?"

Pleased with his accomplishments and thrilled to finally be presented a question he was sure of, Carter informed the Admiral that he finished 5th out of a student body numbering 820. Then he waited for a commendation from the old sailor, but it never came.

Jimmy Carter later recounted the incident.

"Did you always do your best?" was the question that broke the uncomfortable silence between the two men.

Carter thought and then cleared his throat, "No, sir, I did not," was his hesitant reply.

Rickover turned his chair around, signaling the interview was over, and asked, "Why not?"

It's a good question—"Why not?"

How do you evaluate what *you* do? Poor, so-so, adequate, good, very good, outstanding? We are called to be people of excellence, to fulfill our potential. It's easy to coast along rather than make that extra effort. Some men are pretty good at that. But if you can do better, why not?[39]

In what area of your life do you need to follow through more thoroughly? If you need some help figuring that out, ask a friend. Ask one of your children. Better yet, ask your spouse! And next time you tackle a task, keep this in mind: "Whatever you do, work at it with all your heart, as working for the Lord, not for men, since you know that you will receive an inheritance from the Lord as a reward. It is the Lord Christ you are serving" (Colossians 3:23–24).

Your accomplishments can draw someone to the Lord. Your growth as a believer can be a witness for Christ. That's an excellent reason to be thorough.

He's Got a Reputation

47

One of my earliest encounters with a smallmouth came at Lake Arrowhead in California. I was flipping a plastic sandworm between a couple of docks when something smashed into the hook and ripped the worm apart. I thought, *What in the world was that?* He about yanked the rod out of my hand! I put on a new worm, flipped it out, and saw a couple of large bluegill go after it. But another shape cut in front, pushed them out of the way, and engulfed my worm as if he hadn't seen food for a year. When I landed him, it was a one-and-a-half-pound smallmouth. He felt like a pike the way he went after the worm. That was my introduction to a tough fighter.

One day I was float tubing over a flat sandy bottom. It was so clear you could see small rocks. You could also see several smallmouth and they didn't spook. When the sandworm slid by they ripped into it. The smaller ones were left behind. The bigger the fish the more aggressive it seemed.

Smallmouth have a reputation. They're tough. They're the bullies in the pond. They're like the street fighter on an ice hockey team. When you put a smallmouth in a tank with other fish, even those larger than the smalley, it's no contest. He'll dominate the tank. It's like he has a vendetta against the others and becomes the marshal from Dodge City. Some say this tendency is in its genes. Unfortunately, I've run into anglers who reminded me of the smallmouth. If anyone questions their actions, they claim, "That's just the way I am. I was born this way." Who do you know that resembles a smallmouth in personality?

Some say noise and commotion draw these bass in more than other species because they're so curious. One writer said, "They'll bite things they shouldn't, even when they know better." If a smallmouth had hands, it would be smacking itself on the side of the head, saying, "I knew I shouldn't have bit that." So to appeal to their curious nature, use noisy brass sinkers, run the outboard and rile up the bottom, use crackle and Alka-Seltzer in a tube and toss the tube out to make noise, use large spinnerblades, and, above all, rattles.

Smallmouth tend to be gregarious. Sometimes they seem to hunt for food as a team. The smaller ones will drive the food out from where it's hiding and a larger one will nail the food. And yet at times the larger one forages for the smaller one.

So if you want to catch smallmouth, make some noise and feed their curiosity.[40]

Just as certain species have reputations, so do people. Think about it for a minute. What was your reputation as a child? As a teenager? What is it now? Everyone has one. It's what people think about you. When you get a reputation, it's kind of difficult to change it, especially if it's bad. Just look at some of those in the limelight—entertainers, athletes, or even presidents. If your reputation is good, all it takes is one slip and it's tarnished.

Most people I know don't purposely change their reputation. But I do know one who did. And it was for a good reason.

> Who, although being essentially one with God and in the form of God [possessing the fullness of the attributes which make God God], did not think this equality with God was a thing to be eagerly grasped or retained; but stripped Himself [of all privileges and rightful dignity] so as to assume the guise of a servant (slave), in that He became like men and was born a human being. And after He had appeared in human form He abased and humbled Himself [still further] and carried His obedience to the extreme of death, even the death of [the] cross! (Philippians 2:6–8 AMP)

"Stripped himself" in another version says, "He made himself of no reputation" (NKJV).

Why? For you. For me. For the entire world—He gave up what He had to reach out and give *us* an opportunity to have a new reputation. It's much better to be known (or have the reputation) as a Christian—one who knows Christ, loves Him, serves Him, and follows Him. If that's the only reputation I have in life . . . it's good enough.

A new commandment I give to
you, that you love one another,
even as I have loved you, that you
also love one another. By this all
men will know that you are My
disciples, if you have love for one
another.

—*John 13:34–35* NASB

Your Bass Weighed How Much?

48

*Y*ou could hear the two anglers from several hundred yards away. Every time they boated a bass, one would say, "Look at the size of that fish! This is great."

As I cruised by I asked how it was going. They said, "Man, we've hit a school of good ones. Every fish has been over three pounds." And they held up their latest catch for me to see before they released it. The problem was, it didn't look like any three-pounder I'd ever seen (and I tend to be a stickler for accuracy, especially when it comes to fish).

I stopped a good distance away and immediately tied into a

bass. Once it was boated, one of them yelled over, "I see you found that school too."

I said, "Looks like it." They watched as I took out my digital scales to weigh it, since I was curious as to what it really weighed. Right at a pound and a half. I was sort of hoping they wouldn't ask what it weighed, but they did. When I told them, they were good sports and said, "I guess we were off a bit. Oh well, we'll just revise our guesstimate downward. At least they're still a lot of fun." And that they were.

Weight used to be important. But weight can vary depending on the scale, since very few scales are certified. Today there's more emphasis on length. An inch is an inch. A problem arises when you try to use length to determine weight. A twenty-one-inch bass could weigh five, six, or even seven pounds. Some fish look as though they've been to Weight Watchers, while others are virtual food machines in appearance. I fish one lake where most of the bass look underfed and undernourished and another where they resemble footballs. And as you would guess, the bigger the bass, the more weight it gains for each inch it grows.

Studies show a considerable variation of weight even at a given length. For example, the average twenty-two-inch bass from Florida weighs about six-and-a-half pounds, which is similar to the standard weight. But surveys conducted by biologists found bass that length that weighed as little as four-and-a-half pounds to as heavy as eight pounds. That's quite a variation.

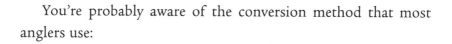

You're probably aware of the conversion method that most anglers use:

$$\frac{\text{Length} \times \text{girth} \times \text{girth}}{800} = \text{weight}$$

This works for some fish, but not very well with those that are almost as round as they are long. Biologists in California have developed a formula that seems to work better on bass that are longer than twenty-two inches with a girth over twenty-one inches:

$$\frac{\text{Length} \times \text{length} \times \text{girth}}{1000} = \text{weight}$$

Even so, it's still not 100 percent accurate. Perhaps you've heard about Bob Crupi of California. (Bob also guides, and I've gone on several trips with him. Not only did I catch huge bass but I also learned much from his years of experience.) He's the only one who's landed two bass over twenty pounds. He weighed his 1991 fish on a certified scale and it came out at 22.01 pounds. Using the new formula, however, it would have come in at 23.9. That would have been a world record. Unfortunately, it wasn't.

You may want to use these formulas to get a general idea. That's better than eyeballing your bass and then (unconsciously, of course) throwing on a couple of pounds for good measure. But the best way is to get a good digital scale (and get it certified).[41]

There's something else more important that we need to be accurate about: what the Scripture really means. I've seen people take verses out of context and totally warp their meaning. Others have misinterpreted passages to fit their own bias or support their point. Some are enamored with a certain translation, even though it may not be the most accurate. It may help to read (or even memorize) the following to make sure you're on track:

> But you should continue following the teachings you learned. You know they are true, because you trust those who taught you. Since you were a child you have known the Holy Scriptures, which are able to make you wise. And that wisdom leads to salvation through faith in Christ Jesus. All Scripture is given by God and is useful for teaching, for showing people what is wrong in their lives, for correcting faults, and for teaching how to live right. Using the Scriptures, the person who serves God will be capable, having all that is needed to do every good work. (2 Timothy 3:14–17 NCV)

We're also called to be an accurate reflection of Jesus. It's easy to either misrepresent Him or distort Him. Our calling is to let Him have control of our life. When we do, we can then let Jesus live through us and really reflect who He is and what He's done for us. Then people won't question whether or not we're Christians as I questioned the weight of those "three-pound" bass.

Do You Remember?

49

The year was 1941. It was summer, so the attack on Pearl Harbor had not yet taken place. My parents, brother, and I had taken the train from Los Angeles to Flint, Michigan, to pick up a new Chevrolet (for only $700! *Groan*). We then drove to South Dakota and Iowa to visit relatives. And while we were there I had a life-changing experience—fishing. It was an exciting new world to a four-year-old boy from California. My cousins and brother and I went down to a little creek and fished for something they called chubs. We filled a bucket with them and took them back to the house. I can still recall a picture of that experience. I was hooked! Fishing was the greatest.

Since we lived in Southern California, ocean fishing became a family activity. Back then we used long cane poles, and at times we'd swing barracuda, bonita, and mackerel up onto the deck of a barge. Often we fished in the same way off the Santa Monica Pier.

I've never forgotten one particular outing on the pier. I was fishing with my parents, and a teenage boy asked if he could have some mackerel for bait. Later on I looked over the other side of the pier and said, "Mom, look. That boy is swimming now." He was floating face down and there was blood in the water. He wasn't swimming. He'd been fishing from the rafters and pilings under the pier and apparently had hit his head on a beam and fallen into the water. I watched the rescue and remember my parents' admonition to be careful even when you're fishing.

What do you remember about your first fishing experiences? Have you thought about them recently? Have you shared those memories with your friends or family?

I remember my daughter's first ocean fishing experience. (Some of it I'd like to forget!) She was five and already quite independent. She wanted to catch her own anchovy out of the bait tank, put it on the hook, and toss it in the water. And she did. Three barracuda came on deck because of her efforts. But a problem emerged. Earlier, on the drive down to the waterfront, Sheryl had asked a simple question: "Daddy, if I catch a shark, can I take it home to Mommy?" Now, either I had spaced out, was asleep, or thought, *fat chance of that happening*, because I said, "Sure you can."

Two hours later she's got a six-foot shark on her line! Now there are two versions of the outcome. I *distinctly* remember, in fact I'm *absolutely* sure the shark broke the line. Sheryl says I cut the line. I have *no recollection* of that whatsoever. (I didn't have a death wish either. Can you imagine the look on my wife's face if we'd walked through the door with a six-foot shark! "You brought home what?") Memories are a big part of our lives.

Do you remember the first bass you caught? I hope so. That was the beginning of an important chapter in your life. I remember a small lake in Montana—Lake Mary Ronan. I'd fished most of the day for kokanee salmon and decided to try for a bass. A storm was coming over the mountain. I could hear the thunder and see some rain squalls. I flipped that frog-colored Hula Popper next to some reeds. The water exploded and he inhaled it. He was the first . . . but not the last.

It's great to have these memories. And remembering is a good thing. Sometimes in trying to live the Christian life we forget things that we need to remember and refer to so that our life stays on the right track. For example, do you remember when you first met the Lord? Do you remember the first time you experienced God's working in your life or leading you in some way?

The Scriptures call us to remember.

In John 15, Jesus told His disciples, "Remember what I told you" (v. 20 NCV). What did He tell them? It may help you to take out your Bible and read John 15:1–20.

Another passage tells us, "You have left the love you had in the beginning. So remember where you were before you fell" (Revelation 2:4–5 NCV).

It's easy to let our relationship with Jesus fade. It won't, if each day we remember

who Jesus is;
what He's done for us; and
how much He loves us.

Remembering these truths can be life-changing.

Do not set foot on the path of the wicked or walk in the way of evil men. Avoid it, do not travel on it; turn from it and go on your way.

—Proverbs 4:14–15

It's Dangerous Out There

50

$\mathcal{E}$very fishing locale has its own built-in dangers. They come in many forms: unexpected weather changes, a sunken snag that rips a hole in the bottom of your boat, even animals. Yes, animals. Have you ever had bees drive you away from a prime fishing spot? It can happen, and it did happen. My nephew and I were walking the Jocco River in Montana. As we worked our way along the bank, we saw a couple of likely spots just ahead. We pushed through the bushes and cast out, not realizing the spot was already taken … by a number of unhappy, grudge-carrying bees. We didn't argue. Sorry, but fish aren't worth bee stings, especially when you're allergic to them.

What about bears? We went downstream a mile, rounded a bend, and found a great spot. Across from us was a large patch of wild berry bushes. It seemed strange that a number of these thorny bushes were shaking when there was no wind. All of a sudden a big black head popped out of the bushes about thirty-five feet away and looked right at us. Then a second head emerged with the same stare. A third popped out and gave a grunt. It was the proverbial three bears, but this time it was a mom and her cubs. We thought, *This is our fishing hole—beat it, bears!* The bears thought, *This is our berry patch; the river isn't that wide or deep, so get lost, people!* We did. Being watched and evaluated as a possible meal somehow takes the fun out of fishing.

What about fleas? That's right, fleas! My wife, Joyce, and I were fishing off a sandy beach on Yellowstone Lake on our anniversary a number of years ago. The fish were going wild. The sun got hotter, and I took off my shirt, laid it on the sand, and kept casting. When we finished, I put the shirt back on, and we drove back to our cabin in Grand Teton National Park. When I took the shirt off to take a shower, I was shocked. My upper body was covered with scores of bites—flea bites. The fleas in the sand hitchhiked on the shirt to get a free ride and free meal. So we spent a few hours dabbing calamine lotion all over my body. I can think of better ways to spend an anniversary afternoon!

And then there are snakes. A snake can ruin the best day of fishing. An angler out on Lake Irvine stopped his boat one morning and stood on one of the seats in the back. That's not too unusual. I've seen a number do this off the shoreline as they cast for bass. But he was in the middle of the lake, had no rod in hand, and was yelling his head off. It seemed a rattler had crawled into the boat the night before, and when the sun came out and warmed his body, he came alive. So did the boatman. Fortunately, someone came along and bailed out the snake.

I was fishing largemouth with a guide at Euchi Lake in Oklahoma in the early springtime. Foliage was just starting to fill in the thick forest and heavy undergrowth around the lake. The guide's instructions were interesting: "If you cast a plastic or even an expensive lure or spinnerbait on the shore and hang it up, just break it off. We don't retrieve them." That seemed strange, and a bit expensive, especially when the lures were in plain sight. He went on to describe an experience with a client who struck a log on shore with a ten-to-fifteen-dollar lure. He wanted to retrieve it in the worst way. The guide said, "Well, we can do that if you all are set on gettin' it back, but what're you goin' to do with that cottonmouth sittin' next to it?"

Our guide went on to say that the shoreline was so infested with snakes that he never got out of the boat. Good advice. Sometimes you need to protect yourself, so you make preparations by checking out the terrain, asking advice of locals, keeping your eyes open, or carrying something in case you're attacked. Like pepper spray. My friend bought some, and as we exited his car in his garage, he pulled it out and read the instructions. But he went a step further. He decided to test it . . . in the garage. He walked away from the car, sprayed it, and walked back. A couple of minutes later he walked across the garage right through the spray that was just hanging in the air. After he quit coughing, sneezing, and having his eyes water, Gary said, "Man, that stuff works." As I opened my mouth to make a kind remark, I breathed some of it in—and got out of there. Don't test it inside. It's worse than some of those critters out there.

Sometimes you need to protect yourself against other things in life as well.

People can give you bad advice.

People can tempt you.

Satan can tempt you.

Just as you stay away from bees, fleas, bears, and snakes, keep yourself from everyday dangers.

God's Word says to get away from temptations: "Flee the evil desires of youth, and pursue righteousness, faith, love and peace, along with those who call on the Lord out of a pure heart" (2 Timothy 2:22). What do *you* need to run from?

God's Word also says, "For we do not have a high priest who is unable to sympathize with our weaknesses, but we have one who has been tempted in every way, just as we are—yet was without sin. Let us then approach the throne of grace with confidence, so that we may receive mercy and find grace to help us in our time of need" (Hebrews 4:15–16).

There's your protection. It's available. All you have to do is ask.

Just as you stay away from bees, fleas, bears, and snakes, keep yourself from everyday dangers.

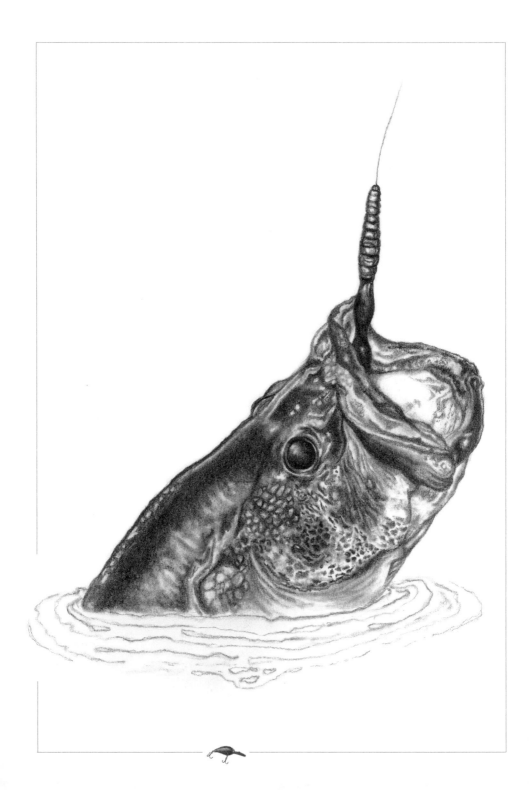

What's All This About a Full Moon?

"The moon? That's an old wives' tale. It has no impact on catching bass."

"Man, I read those lunar tables like they're the Gospel itself. That's how I know when to go fishing."

"Anyone knows during a full moon, with all that bright light, the bass are feeding all night. That's why they don't bite."

I've heard these and many other theories about the moon and fishing. Some swear by the moon tables, while others debunk the whole idea.

I discovered Bill Murphy's helpful thoughts about the lunar tables and the moon phases in his book *In Pursuit of the Giant Bass*. He doesn't follow lunar tables, but uses the moon phases to get the best day and then fishes all day to get the best bite.

Now, here is an angler who from 1970 to 1992 caught thirty-nine largemouth between thirteen and seventeen pounds each. He's caught hundreds in the eight-to-ten-pound class. He knows what he's talking about. You may be surprised by his results and the correlation with the moon. He's been keeping detailed records since 1970. Almost 70 percent of his eight-pound-plus bass were taken during full-moon cycles. And almost 75 percent of his ten-pound-plus fish were caught on either a waxing (rising) or a waning (setting) phase of the full-moon cycle. Now, that got my attention! I'm looking at the moon phases with a new perspective.

Bill Murphy suggested that sometimes the bass have fed so heavily during the waxing phase that when the full moon arrives the fish are already full. That's why they don't hit as well. So fishing during a full moon could be similar to fishing on the backside of a frontal system. The fish have had their meal. They're satisfied, so why hit anything else? He also suggests that the fishing may not be as good on the three-fourths waxing moon as the waning.

I like his flexibility. This is *his* experience, but he allows differences to exist. He suggests that successful moon fishing is just a matter of identifying the moon 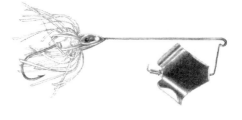 phases that best suit your style of angling. It boils down to personal technique and areas fished, which is why some anglers like certain moon phases while others don't. It's possible to catch large bass on any moon phase, and "those anglers who are successful have programmed their own success to certain moon phase patterns just as I have done." That allows for different perspectives, and I like that in a successful angler rather than the attitude "This is my way of doing it. It's the best way, and it's the only way."

You may not believe in this moon stuff at all. You may be a diehard believer and have your own theories. Wherever you are, consider reading this book. What Bill Murphy says will challenge your thinking.⁴²

After you read it, when darkness settles in and the moon begins to rise on the horizon, you may find yourself looking at the moon in a new way and thinking, *I wonder what those bass are doing now? Is this a waxing or waning moon? Hmm, maybe those big ones are cruising into the shallows. I wonder . . .*

We take the moon for granted. It's just there. We've sent spacecraft and men up there. We've even got a flag sitting on it. We think we own it. We don't. God does. It's His creation.

The psalmist talked about the moon:

> When I consider your heavens, the work of your fingers, the moon and the stars, which you have set in place. . . . (Psalm 8:3)
> The moon marks off the seasons, and the sun knows when to go down. (Psalm 104:19)
> Give thanks to the Lord of lords . . . who made the great lights—*His love endures forever*. The sun to govern the day, *His love endures forever*. The moon and stars govern the night; *His love endures forever*. (Psalm 136:3, 7–9, emphasis added)

We see the moon. We bask in its light. It's tied into romantic themes. I've heard some guys tell their wives, "Hey, honey, we got a romantic full moon tonight. What say we crank up the ol' bass boat for a while and cruise the lake, just you and me?" Yeah, right. The bass may fall for that line, but I doubt if your wife will.

Take another look at the moon tonight. What do you see? What do you think of? Bass, or God's creation? Enjoy its light. One day that light will be gone. That's what Jesus said:

> Immediately after the distress of those days "the sun will

be darkened, and the moon will not give its light; the stars will fall from the sky, and the heavenly bodies will be shaken." At that time the sign of the Son of Man will appear in the sky, and all the nations of the earth will mourn. They will see the Son of Man coming on the clouds of the sky, with power and great glory." (Matthew 24:29–30)

Let's be ready for His coming.

The Newest Rig—Changing the Face of Bass Fishing

52

few years ago in a faraway country, there was developed a new technique that is making an impact on bass fishing. It's a very versatile rig. You can use it to fish practically any type of structure and cover. What do you call this rig? That depends. You could call it the "always lucky" rig, for that's what the Japanese name means. Or you could call it "stacking" or an "upside-down Carolina rigging" or "suspend doodle system" or "down-shot!" You've probably heard it referred to as "drop-shot."

Whatever you call it, this rig works.

It was developed in Japan, and it's simple. This rig has a weight on the bottom of the line with the hook tied directly to the line (using a palomar knot) from a few inches to a couple of feet up from the weight.

You can use it in deep water or shallow water. And what makes it work is your line control and presentation. You can work this rig vertically like a jig or cast it to the base of a tree and wiggle it in place. It will work brush piles, high underwater grass, or fallen timber. Don't use it when you have aggressive fish or muddy water. But if you've got the problem of clear water or fish with an attitude (they're negative or have a "whatever," could-care-less frame of mind), the drop-shot could shake up their lives.

Some think this technique is like the old jig bit. It's not. It's a subtle finesse technique. Someone said it's like doodling with patience. You make a cast, or drop it straight down until the weight hits the bottom. Then you stay in place and shake. That's the key, shaking. Sometimes you take up to five minutes for each cast.

Subtle shakes and lifts, not intense, violent gyrations, are what attract the bass. You want your bait to dance and hover in place. Because you're fishing straight down, the better drop-shot baits have a straight, paddle, or forked tail. Plain tails are more active when you fish them vertically. Most of today's drop-shot baits are small, anywhere from three to five inches, and color is important. They tend to be translucent with slight, subtle colors or glitter.

Your line is important. If you use heavy line, get ready to make a change. In Japan the finesse angler sometimes uses two-pound line to entice bass. Four-pound is standard for them. Those on the United States West Coast favor six- to eight-pound test, green, brown, or clear. Some have latched on to the new fluorocarbon lines.[43]

Well, there you have a brief introduction to a new approach

that some say is changing the face of bass fishing. It's both interesting and exciting.

There's something else that has brought about a change. In fact, it has changed the face of history permanently. It's called *Christianity*. And through the church, the world is changed. Recently I found a book titled *How God Saved Civilization*. This is what the author says:

> Civilization has no hope. No hope at all, except through God. God alone can preserve a person, a family, a people group, a nation or any part of civilization that's worth preserving. Without God, no one, no culture can survive. In fact, left to itself, civilization self-destructs.
>
> That's the bad news. But the good news is that God does love the world and preserves it from experiencing its own complete self-destruction. Through the inexplicable gift of his Son, Jesus, God extends His love. And before Jesus left planet earth, He launched one of God's best ideas: the Church. For some mysterious reason, God chose to accomplish His kingdom through the Church. Through the true Church, He preserves us from inevitable self-destruction. Beginning 2000 years ago, the Church has preserved and passed on the gospel, praying that people will open their hearts to receive it so that when civilization as we know it "does" end, God's people will all be gathered, ready to receive Him.[44]

That really *is* good news. It's easy for many of us to share the newest info that we've learned about catching bass with others. But who have you told about the good news of Jesus? If you know Him, share Him with others. Everyone benefits from that kind of sharing.

A sluggard does not plow in season; so at harvest time he looks but finds nothing.

—Proverbs 20:4

Is It Always This Easy?

53

$\mathcal{F}$ork Lake. Most of us who have been bass fishing for any length of time have heard stories about this lake. It's got a reputation. And it deserves one. The number of bass over ten pounds caught there is astounding.

A guide shared an experience with me that he could have done without. It seems that a man met a woman in a hotel bar in San Diego. The program on the bar's TV described the fishing at Fork Lake in Texas. All it took was one comment from the woman—"I'd sure love to go fishing there"—and the man said, "Let's do it." They weren't even sure where Fork Lake was, but figured if they could fly into Dallas, they'd locate it. They asked around, rented a car, arrived at the lake, and found a guide. They made the arrangements for the next morning, but before they parted, the guide told them to bring some warm clothes. He was surprised when he heard back, "Hey, this is all we have . . . just what you see on us." So the guide said he'd bring some extra stuff with him. He brought a coat for the man and a sleeping bag for his lady friend, since she didn't look like she would take to the rigors of the weather or fishing.

When they hit the first cove, he gave the man the rod and instructed him what to do: "When the fish hits, set the hook as hard as you can." He knew it was going to be a long day when he heard in reply, "What's that mean, set the hook?" I can just imagine the look on the guide's face, the thoughts that went through his mind, and what he was tempted to say. He kept his cool, gave some more instruction, and went to fishing. An hour later the San Diego man had boated a ten-pounder. An hour later an eleven-pounder came aboard, which led the guy to ask a profound question: "Hey, is catching these big bass always this easy?" Now, there's a death wish question. I know guides who have fished twenty years and are still working on their first double-digit bass.

The couple probably went back to San Diego and spread a distorted view of bass fishing all around town. Of course, any fishing experiences after one like that are all downhill.

This guy is like many others who believe everything in life ought to come easy. They don't spend time learning, practicing, improving their skill, or working hard. Their motto is, "If it doesn't come easy, it ain't worth it."

Look at what the book of Proverbs says about this type of individual:

> I went past the field of the sluggard, past the vineyard of the man who lacks judgment; thorns had come up everywhere, the ground was covered with weeds, and the stone wall was in ruins. (Proverbs 24:30–31)

How long will you lie there, you sluggard? When will you get up from your sleep? A little sleep, a little slumber, a little folding of the hands to rest—and poverty will come on you like a bandit and scarcity like an armed man. (Proverbs 6:9–11)

The Bible calls this person a sluggard; this is the guy who may not start things, or he may not finish them. Some are selectively lazy. They're workhorses at the office, and that's good. Whatever we do ought to be done for the Lord's sake.

Since more men than women are probably reading this book, we'll talk about men right now.

Men, let's take a detour away from work and go to the home front. What does your garage look like? What about the workroom, the backyard, or the catchall drawer in the kitchen? If you're married, how would your wife rate you on productivity around the homestead? Yeah, you're right. Bad question! But necessary to ask. Why? Simply because a number of men have MPP—Multiple Personality Problem. They're super-charged workhorses on the job, but at home they function like sluggards. And to make matters worse (much worse!), if their wives know they're giving their all at the office, they will not be happy receiving only the leftovers at home.

So what's the answer? Consistent productivity—at work and at home. Laziness is not a spiritual gift or calling. Scripture calls us to do our best and to give our best—everywhere. Is it easy? No. Attainable? Definitely.

*Some people don't seem to get the
message that they can't control
everything; they keep trying.*

Are You Really in Control?

Most anglers want to be in control. You can see it in the way they walk to the dock or launch their boat. It's evident in what they say and how they say it. What they really want is to be in control of their fishing. To some degree we can be in charge. We can buy the best equipment, keep it in the best repair, sharpen our hooks, retie our knots periodically, and study bass. This much we can control.

But once our bait hits the water, we have little control as to when the fish hits, how hard, and where. The big issue is who's in control once that bass hits. We want to control him, but he wants to control us. So what we have is one big power struggle. Some anglers land almost all the fish they hook. They're in control. Others lose more than they land because they let the bass control them.

What's the best way to control a bass? Shaw Grigsby suggests the following:

1. Try to keep him from changing directions.
2. If he runs through heavy cover, let him run.
3. Keep him in view so you can react.
4. Don't do anything else when you're fighting a fish.
5. Keep him down in the water.
6. Don't relax when he gets close to the boat.
7. Expect him to try to jump at the boat.[45]

Following these simple suggestions can give us more control, but realize there are many aspects of fishing—as well as life—we'll never be able to control, no matter how hard we try.

But some people don't seem to get the message that they can't control everything; they keep trying. Why? Because they must be in control of every aspect of their lives. They push, pull, persuade, manipulate, and withdraw. Yes, withdraw. Silence and withdrawal are great ways to control others. They even try to control cats. Have you ever tried to control a cat? It's a losing battle. There's just no way to accomplish that feat. Cats have incorrigible character disorders.

What prompts this lifestyle?

Control is a camouflage for fear. Who wants to be afraid or even admit that you are? Not I. Not you. Fear makes us feel vulnerable: If others knew we were afraid they'd take advantage of us. So we hide our fear by going on the offensive.

"There is no fear in love. But perfect love drives out fear, because fear has to do with punishment. The one who fears is not made perfect in love. We love because he first loved us" (1 John 4:18–19).

Control is a cover-up for security. A secure person doesn't need to be always in control. He can defer to others, ask their advice, be comfortable when someone else leads. To feel safe we go overboard by trying to control everything and everyone. There's an emptiness within us when we're insecure; we're like a bucket with a hole in it. We can never get filled up, but we keep trying through control.

Control is a cover-up for low self-esteem. When we feel down on ourselves, worthless, or lacking, we don't want others to know about it. And we may even blame them for helping to create the problem. What better way to overcome this than by making others pay through our control? But you know we're fooling ourselves. Control never fulfills, it never solves the basic problem. It simply perpetuates it. It never draws others closer but rather pushes them away. And we end up feeling worse.

Give God the reins of your life. Let Him control you. When God is in control of your life, you'll be amazed at how much better your relationships with others will be.

*The tongue that brings healing is a
tree of life, but a deceitful tongue
crushes the spirit.*

—Proverbs 15:4

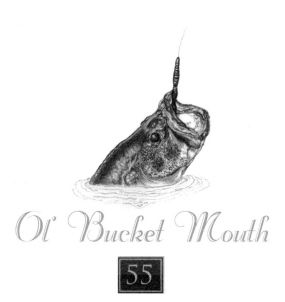

Ol' Bucket Mouth

55

He's called ol' bucket mouth. I've also heard him referred to as a garbage disposal or the terminator. His mouth isn't just big, it's huge. A bass will grab and digest any food that fits the width of its mouth. Lizards, snakes, turtles, and dragonflies go down that throat. But that's not all! Let a mouse or even a rat fall into the water, and it could end up being digested. That's why when you look through the Bass Pro catalog you'll see rat and mouse lures. How about a nice fluffy duckling or a fat frog? Bass love both. One day I was fishing from shore casting a rubber frog onto a patch of green scum and slowly twitching my offering back. Right below where I was standing the scum stopped and the water was clear. I was about three feet above the water and I twitched my frog into the clear water. All of a sudden I saw this steel trap of a mouth ascending from under the water. The movie *Jaws* flashed through my mind. He came straight out of the water, missing the frog, and I swear if he had tonsils I could have counted them. I was so shocked I jumped backward, yelled, and startled a jogger on the adjacent path. (Actually he missed the frog because I jerked it away when he spooked me.) I can tell from firsthand experience that mouth *is* large.

When a bass attacks a school of minnows, he's like a mowing machine in a field of wheat. He likes to swallow his food whole, and he's got an expandable belly (not unlike some others I know). But he's also adept at picking up food off the bottom, using his mouth like tweezers. I've seen bass with red, bruised lips from hitting the rocks as they go after crawdads.

With that mouth, if a bass could talk, he'd probably talk your arm and leg off. He's the fish that would be saying, "Oops, why'd I say that? I stuck my fin in my mouth again." His mouth could get him into trouble. So can ours. Some anglers resemble bass in more ways than one, and it's not always that pleasant. Perhaps that's why Scripture includes so many guidelines about our mouths.

Let me ask you a trivia question: How many times are the words *tongue, mouth, lips,* and *words* mentioned in the book of Proverbs? I'll answer that later, but suffice to say that Proverbs is the finest guide on how to handle the "Largemouth Bass Syndrome." In practical advice it surpasses all the other books in the Bible. Look at the following insights on what *not* to say:

How about boasting? "Like clouds and wind without rain is a man who boasts of gifts he does not give" (Proverbs 25:14). Talk is useless. And when you're a bass angler it's easy to fall into the "can you top this?" discussions about our exploits on the lake. Paul talked about this too: "Do not let any unwholesome talk come out of your mouths, but only what is helpful for building others up according to their needs, that it may benefit those who listen" (Ephesians 4:29).

How about flattery? "He who rebukes a man will in the end gain more favor than he who has a flattering tongue" (Proverbs 28:23). We know how to butter up someone, especially when we want something . . . like learning the favorite spots of the top anglers!

How about verbosity or running off at the mouth? Look at Proverbs 10:19 (TLB): "Don't talk so much. You keep putting your foot in your mouth. Be sensible and turn off the flow!" That's graphic! You've met people like this; they fill the air with words—empty words of no significance—to impress others.

Avoid angry, argumentative words. "An angry man stirs up dissension, and a hot-tempered one commits many sins" (Proverbs 29:22). Strife implies rigidity, stubbornness, and unhealthy anger. An angry angler isn't a pleasant picture.

If you'd like some other helpful guidelines, read Proverbs 14:6–7; 17:14; James 3:1–18. And these are just starters. Which verses would help you if you applied them?

By the way, the answer to the trivia question is: more than one hundred fifty times!

There's a law written somewhere that says a big fish will hit while you're pouring a cup of coffee.

How to Lose a Fish–Part 1

$\mathcal{Y}$ou're probably saying, "I don't need any help losing fish, thank you. I can lose plenty on my own." We've all lost them. I wonder, though, how many we could have avoided losing. Instead of kicking yourself and grumbling, "If only I'd . . ." you can be proactive and take some preventative steps to reduce the number of lost fish.

Let's look at the best ways to *lose* a fish.

Don't check your line. That's a super way to break off a big one. Your line may look good, but it's just like picking a marriage partner: looks aren't everything. Run the line between your thumb and forefinger and look at it. Get rid of that frayed line. A frayed line means a lost fish. I've got a cupboard with spool after spool, and my lines are changed several times a year.

Use a dull hook. Remember, that bass's mouth is only gristle in some spots. A hook needs to be razor sharp. If not, that dull hook could end up in part of *your* body when he throws it back at you.

Fish in brush. Brush to a bass is like a death penalty pardon from the governor. If brush is there, he'll go for it. Don't let him get there. Fish smart. Work him toward open water. There's nothing more maddening than looking down and seeing that six-to-eight-pound line wrapped around the brush pile.

Use light line. I remember a trip when a guide handed me the wrong rod. We wondered why fish kept breaking off, until he checked and discovered the rod had six-pound line. We made a change, and I landed my next fish—a nine-pounder. For every decrease you make in the strength of the line, the more advantage you give to the bass. If the bass are spooky, though, you may need to go lighter.

Give him some slack. Your fish doesn't need more than an inch in order to escape. I've seen so many anglers set the hook, then give two feet of slack and wonder what happened to that bass. The word is *tight* lines. If your fish comes to the surface, drop the tip but keep the line tight. This may keep him from jumping, and then again, it may not.

Don't pay attention. Doing something else at the same time is a great way to end up kicking yourself. There's a law written somewhere that says a big fish will hit when you're preoccupied. Pouring a cup of coffee, reaching for a snack, dialing your cell phone (these ought to be banned from boats), watching other anglers, opening the live well to check on the fish—these are all distractions that bass love. Keep focused.

Give the big bass all the time he wants. You do that and you'll never see him in your boat. If he's big, put the pressure on, because the longer it takes, the more the advantage shifts in his favor. Your job is to use more muscle than he does and to let him know that he's coming your way.

Get overly excited and pump that adrenaline. You've seen it. The guy is ready to celebrate before the bass is boated. And in his excitement he makes a major error. No more bass. I was watching a pro bass video. The guy landed the largest bass he'd ever caught. In his excitement he held it up without a proper grip and it flipped back into the water before he could measure it. That's also the first time I've heard words bleeped out on a pro's video.

Set your hook like a wimp. Pull that rod back for all it's worth. Think about this. If your hook is embedded in a plastic worm, you've got to get the hook through the worm as well as into the fish. Go ahead, bend your knees, and set it with authority. How many times have you said, "You didn't set the hook, right?" We've all made this mistake.[46]

So which of these do you identify with most? In which area could you improve? (By the way, I'm not done yet. In the next chapter I'll give you some more.)

Losing a bass is a part of fishing, although an unpleasant one. There are other things you can lose in life or lose out on. These too involve a number of avoidable steps. Can you think of any of these areas or steps? Jot them down. Then read on. You may be surprised where all this leads.

The Lord is patient with you, not wanting anyone to perish, but everyone to come to repentance.

—*2 Peter 3:9*

How to Lose a Fish–Part 2

57

$\mathcal{H}$ere are several more ways to lose a bass:

Keep your drag loose. What a great way to avoid a good hook set, give a bass his way, and get yourself upset. Trying to adjust the drag after a fish hits is difficult, plus you don't know how much pressure is on your line. Some are afraid of breaking the line, but if it's fifteen-to-twenty-pound test, that's not too likely. In the Southern California lakes, we often use eight pound, but we let the rod do the work.

Stay in one spot in the boat. In some boats you can't move. But if it's a bass boat, follow that fish. Go to the stern or run to the bow. Step on your lunch (or your partner's) if you have to, but move if a big one's on your line.

Let your bass get to your anchor or motor. To a bass these things are brush. They're something to get into to give him an advantage.

Follow your fish and if necessary put your rod tip low in the water so he can't tangle your line. I had a large bass go under the anchor rope, so I just passed the rod under the line and worked him on the other side. This only works if you're anchored properly with each line out at a slant.

Misuse your net. I've seen it happen. Don't hit the fish on the head with the net and expect him to like it. Have you ever practiced using your net? Few have. Spend several minutes practicing on floating objects and talking with your fishing partner ahead of time, and it will pay dividends later. When the fish is tired or you're bringing him in fast, don't chase after him, beating the water with your net. Let him come to you, and then slide that net under him.[47]

You probably can think of many other ways to lose a fish. Perhaps there's nothing new here, but it helps to be reminded of the basics even if you're a veteran angler, just as each year during spring training baseball's millionaire superstars start with the basics.

I hope you won't lose so many fish. And I hope you remember the basics for some other areas of your life, so that you cut your losses there as well.

Many people are winners in some areas of life but losers in others. What's unfortunate is that their losses don't need to occur. Consider a couple of areas. One of them is marriage. One way to lose your marriage is to be a workaholic—giving all your energies at your workplace and coming home with none left for your family.

Another way to weaken your marriage is not to take the time to discover your spouse's needs and seek to meet them. Do you know how your wife wants you to show your love for her? Is it time, touch, words of affection, acts of service, or gifts? Go ahead, ask. You may be surprised.

You can lose a quality relationship in your marriage or even the marriage itself by not learning how to speak your spouse's language and not learning to celebrate each other's differences. So you're really different from each other. What's new? That's not a negative, unless you make it one. You can cause your spouse to lose her love for you by being a controller, an angry person, or never responding with emotional intimacy.

The second area of life you could lose out on is even more crucial. You could miss experiencing the fullness of this life as well as eternal life by not responding to the gift that God has extended to you. All you need to do is to respond with a simple *yes*. Jesus himself said, "For the Son of man has come to seek and save that which was lost" (Luke 19:10 NASB).

"For God so loved the world that he gave his one and only Son, that whoever believes in him shall not perish but have eternal life" (John 3:16).

This is a loss anyone can prevent by a response that will change your life forever!

My soul finds rest in God alone; my salvation comes from him. He alone is my rock and my salvation; he is my fortress, I will never be shaken.

—Psalm 62:1–2

Flying and Turbulence Go Together

58

Sometimes you have to fly to get to the better fishing experiences. I've flown in small planes to get to lakes in the Yukon, as well as other parts of Canada, Alaska, and some of the lower forty-eight states. I've flown through fog and rain where the bush pilot relied on a GPS to find the right spot. In Alaska we flew not over or around the gigantic snow- and glacier-filled mountains but through them. We felt as though we could reach out and touch the snowfield. The salmon and northern pike we tied into at our destination were worth the trip.

My first flight into the backcountry of Alaska was in a three-passenger Cessna with pontoons. I was in the copilot seat. The pilot came in low and buzzed the lodge so they'd know to take the jet boat downstream to pick us up. And before he landed, the pilot tilted the plane as he made a turn so that I was looking out the side window straight down at the ground. I didn't like it one bit! So I laughed. It was one of those nervous laughs. I mean, what else could I do—say, "Knock it off, I'm scared"? The pilot looked over and said, "Hey, you like that, huh?" and proceeded to do it again! No, I *didn't* like it, huh!

Have *you* flown much? If so, you probably have a few experiences to relate, some of which *you* could do without. Like the time lightning struck next to the plane and the thunderclap made me think we'd just lost an engine. (I could have done without that one. My wife never batted an eyelash. I did more than that!) Or the times the air was rough—really rough—with the 747 bouncing all over the sky, trays spilling, and people throwing up. Or it may have been a continuous bumping for two hours that kept you in your seat without being able to take that needed trip to the bathroom. That rough air has a name: turbulence.

Bad weather and turbulence are just part of flying. It's possible to avoid some of it, but there are times when you can't get around it or over it. You've got to go through it until you get to the calm air on the other side. This sounds a bit like the journey of life, doesn't it? Did you know there are four degrees of turbulence? Light, moderate, severe, and extreme. When your coffee jiggles, you're in light turbulence; when it spills, you're in moderate. Pilots make every attempt to avoid severe and extreme.

In life there will be turbulence. If you want to totally avoid it, do what the pilot does: stay on the ground and go nowhere. As you go through light and moderate turbulence you have an opportunity to grow and become different, more Christlike, because of the experience. This turbulence can refine you. But just as severe and extreme turbulence can cause structural damage to the plane or injure passengers, it can do the same to you. What does a pilot do when encountering extreme turbulence? He slows down. There'll be a rough ride, but slowing down eliminates some of the risk.

What can you do to slow down and lessen the risk of damage that occurs in life's turbulence?

> Be careful for nothing; but in every thing by prayer and supplication with thanksgiving let your requests be made known unto God. And the peace of God, which passeth all understanding, shall keep your hearts and minds through Christ Jesus. Finally, brethren, whatsoever things are true, whatsoever things are honest, whatsoever things are just, whatsoever things are pure, whatsoever things are lovely, whatsoever things are of good report; if there be any virtue, and if there be any praise, think on these things. Those things, which ye have both learned, and received, and heard, and seen in me, do: and the God of peace shall be with you. (Philippians 4:6–9 KJV)

You could stop and ask, "Am I running ahead of God, or

allowing Him to set the pace in my life?" Some people have a pacemaker for their heart. God is the pacemaker for our lives. The psalmist said, "Be still and rest in the Lord; wait for Him, and patiently stay yourself upon Him" (Psalm 37:7 AMP).

too fast an approach to their beds or by making noise. One morning while float tubing a small lake for smallmouth, I put it all together. I could see them on sand and gravel. Using a sidearm motion to flip the plastic worm, I avoided a lot of overhead arm movement. When a bass sees that arm and rod in motion he has one response—*git!* The sun was also behind me, making it easier to see the fish underwater. When I found this hot spot, I didn't yell to my fishing partner, I motioned. That's because sound travels well underwater.

I'm no genius. I didn't come up with these insights on my own. I read the book *Bass Master Shaw Grigsby: Notes on Fishing and Life*.[48] It's helped. I like his concept that sight fishing involves both hunting and fishing.

Some are intimidated by sight fishing. It does take practice, skill, and the ability to both look *and* see. Some people look but they don't see. They're sort of blind. In fact, I'm partially blind. So are you. We may have 20/20 or 20/40 vision, but in some ways we're blind. Our view is distorted.

Our ability to perceive life is similar to that of a camera. Photographers can alter the image of reality through the use of various lenses or filters. A wide-angle lens gives a much broader panorama, but the objects appear distant and smaller. A telephoto lens has a narrower and more selective view of life. It can focus on a beautiful flower, but in so doing it shuts out the rest of the garden. A happy, smiling person seen through a fish-eye lens appears distorted and unreal. Filters can change reality, bring darkness into a lighted scene, or even create a mist. Thus a photographic view of the world can be distorted.

It's easy to view your life in a distorted way. Unfortunately, we

What Do You See?

59

Sight fishing. Who comes to mind when you hear that phrase? Usually it's Shaw Grigsby. He's considered the best around. In the 2001 Florida Top 150 Tournament, he used this approach to fishing with a hefty catch of seventy-five pounds, four ounces of bass. We'd all love to have those stringers. He finished in fifth place. Another angler, Dean Rojas, went sight fishing as well. He finished in first place with 108 pounds, including an opening round of five bass weighing forty-five pounds, two ounces! Anglers said they saw huge eight- to ten-pound fish coming in to spawn. The top finishers had bright sunny skies with little wind to help them find bed in the shallow vegetation of Lake Toho. The fish came int hydrilla, Kissimmee grass, and lily pads in two to six feet of wate

But sight fishing doesn't just happen. It takes not only pe sistence but also caution and wisdom. I've spooked many a bass l sometimes distort how we see our spouse, our children, our co-workers, ourselves, and even God. Blindness can be selective, and there can be degrees of it in our lives. What we need is what the blind man received.

> And they came to Bethsaida. And they brought a blind man to [Jesus], and entreated Him to touch him. And taking the blind man by the hand, He brought him out of the village; and after spitting on his eyes, and laying His hands upon him, He asked him, "Do you see anything?" And he looked up and said, "I see men, for I am seeing them like trees, walking about." Then again He laid His hands upon his eyes; and he looked intently and was restored, and began to see everything clearly. (Mark 8:22–25 NASB)

There *is* one person who can open our eyes. It could be we need them opened spiritually more than in any other way.

"I will lead the blind by a way they do not know, in paths they do not know I will guide them. I will make darkness into light before them and rugged places into plains. These are the things I will do, and I will not leave them undone" (Isaiah 42:16 NASB).

How's your eyesight?

ive thanks to the Lord and proclaim his greatness. Let the whole world know what he has done.

—*Psalm 105:1* NLT

The Tribute

60

I went shore fishing the other day and took a friend with me. In fact, I went more for him than for myself. He hadn't been fishing in a while. You see, he's getting old. It's harder for him to get around, and his hearing is going as well. He was quite excited when I told him we were going to the lake. The shore was easier for him than sitting in the old junk boat I keep at this reservoir.

We walked out on an old weed-filled road to the dam, since bass had been schooling there recently. I was bent on getting out there to fish, but my friend seemed to notice the foliage and wildlife around us. I took a cue from him, slowed down, and saw what I'd been missing.

As we sat on the dam I began casting out over the sloping bottom. I alternated between a purple worm and a green fleck Yamamoto spider jig. My friend just sat on a towel, content to watch me catch and release a dozen bass and rattle on about nothing significant. I probably repeated stories he'd heard before, but it didn't bother him like it does some people. Now and then he'd get up and come over to take a closer look at a bass I'd caught. Of course, he's seen many fish in his time. He's even had fish slap him in the head as they were lifted into the boat.

As we walked the half-mile back to the car, I noticed how his pace had slowed. He seemed weary, and it was an effort to get into the van. I told him just to rest while we drove back to the house. We didn't need to talk. I wondered how many more times he'd be able to go fishing with me. I guess we just take it for granted that we'll always be able to fish. Have you ever wondered about that? Most of us just assume nothing will change. I know that one day he won't be able to go. I don't look forward to that day at all.

He's an excellent sight fisherman. He'll spot a bass that I've missed on the shoreline or next to a rock. And he'll stay with that fish until it's caught. What's great about him is the fact that he usually gives me the first opportunity to catch it. Once in a great while he gets a bit impatient and goes for it himself.

He's got an uncanny ability to spot crawdads and other critters under the water too. I've learned a lot from him, and there's still more to learn from him.

My friend has been special in other ways as well.

He came into my life about six months after my son died. For both my wife and me he was a source of comfort during our journey through grief. But we aren't the only ones he's helped. A few years later when my mom was spending her last two months in a convalescent home, I'd visit each day and take my friend with me.

He connected so well with the other residents that some of

them would sit in the lobby for hours waiting to see him. And when they did, their faces, which most of the time had no expression, brightened, and a rare smile emerged. Several would congregate around him, and his gentle touch and silent presence brought delight, comfort, and a bright spot into a day of drab routine. He'd smile at each one and either put his head or a paw in their lap. Sometimes I'd share stories with them about how Sheffield would stalk turtles or crawdads in my small backyard pond. One day he was putting his head under the water up to his ears so I put a snorkel on him and took a series of pictures. They laughed when they thought of a seventy-five-pound golden retriever with a snorkel.

A dog for a friend? You bet! He's more faithful, loyal, patient, and fun-loving than a lot of people I know—as well as never tiring of fishing with me.

Since I'm writing this months before this book will be

published, I don't know if my friend will still be with me by then or not. If he is, I'll be thankful. If he isn't, then I'll have to go on without him. But that's all right. No one can take away the rich memories or experiences we have had together, and for those I am grateful. In fact, for every experience I've had fishing, I'm thankful.

God's Word tells me not to take anything in life for granted. It helps to be reminded:

"In everything give thanks" (1 Thessalonians 5:18 NASB).

"Give thanks to the Lord, for He is good, *His love endures forever*" (Psalm 136:1).

So in thinking of these passages . . .

I'm thankful for living in a country with the freedoms we have.

I'm thankful for all the opportunities I've had to fish.

I'm thankful for the people and animals who have enriched my life. Thank you, Sheffield.

Most of all, I'm thankful that I know who I will spend my future with, both here on earth and when I've left it. I hope you too have that assurance.

"But as many as received Him, to them He gave the right to become children of God, *even* to those who believe in His name" (John 1:12 NASB).

Notes

1. "Smile—You're on TV," Greg Hines, *Bass West* (Nov./Dec. 2000), 12, adapted.
2. "Study's Advice to Husbands: Accept Wife's Influence," by Thomas H. Maught, *Los Angeles Times*, Feb. 22, 1998, Section A, 1.
3. John Ortberg, *Love Beyond Reason* (Grand Rapids, Mich.: Zondervan, 2000), 170–71.
4. Ibid.
5. Max Lucado, *On the Anvil* (Wheaton, Ill.: Tyndale House Publishers, 1985), 69–70.
6. Patrick Morley, *Man in the Mirror* (Brentwood, Tenn.: Wolgemuth and Hyatt, 1989), 274–75.
7. "It Takes More Than a Big Jerk," John Weiss, *The Best of Bassmaster* (Montgomery, Ala.: Bass Anglers Sportsman Society of America, 1987), adapted, 322–25.
8. "SOS Relief," Carol Martens, *Bass West* (Jan. 2001), adapted.
9. "The Feeding Factor: How Much and How Often Does a Bass Eat?" Rich Taylor, *The Best of Bassmaster* (Montgomery, Ala.: Bass Anglers Sportsman Society of America, 1987), adapted, 11–14.
10. A. Cohen, ed., *Proverbs, Soncino Books of the Bible* (London: Soncino Press, 1946), 2.
11. Dr. Keith Jones, "My Fish Is Smarter Than Your Fish," *Bass*

West Magazine, Nov./Dec. 2000, 8–9, adapted.

12. Charles R. Swindoll, *Living On the Ragged Edge* (Waco, Tex.: Word Books, 1985), 218.

13. Gary Richmond, *It's a Jungle Out There* (Eugene, Ore.: Harvest House, 1996), 191.

14. Charles Swindoll, *Come Before Winter* (Portland, Ore.: Multnomah Press, 1985), 138–39.

15. Morley, 215.

16. Don Wirth, "The Evolution of the Trolling Motor," *Bassmaster Magazine* (Mar. 2001), 97–103, adapted.

17. Larry Dahlbert, "Which Hook When," *North American Fisherman* (Mar. 2000), 42–43.

18. Don Wirth, "Hooked on Bass Fishing," *Bassmaster Magazine* (Dec. 2000), 66–67, adapted.

19. Max Lucado, *A Gentle Thunder* (Dallas, Tex.: Word, Inc., 1995), 80–81.

20. Don Wirth, "The Weather and Bass," *Bassmaster* (Apr. 2001), 94–95, adapted.

21. Richard Louv, *Fly-Fishing for Sharks* (New York: Simon & Schuster, 2000), 55–56, adapted.

22. Chuck Swindoll, *Elijah* (Nashville: Word Books, 2000), 121–22.

23. Ross Newhan, "Strike Zone Ordinance," *Los Angeles Times*, March 2, 2001, D1.

24. *Largemouth Bass—An In Fisherman Handbook of Strategies* (Brainerd, Minn.: In Fisherman, 1990), 70–72.

25. Tim Tucker, *Secrets of America's Best Bass Pros* (Tabor City, N.C.: Atlantic Publishing Co., 1991), 204–06, adapted.

26. Original source unknown.

27. Louv, 99–101, adapted.

28. Wayne Cordeiro, *Doing Church As a Team* (Ventura, Calif.: Regal Books, 2000), 90–91, adapted.

29. Shaw Grigsby, *Bass Master Shaw Grigsby* (Washington, D.C.: National Geographic Book, 1998), 131–32, adapted.

30. Ibid., 133, adapted.

31. W. Horace Carter, *How Old Is a Trophy Bass?* (New York: Simon & Schuster, 2000), 56–57, adapted.

32. Dr. James Henshall, *Book of the Black Bass—Scientific and Life History, Together With a Practical Treatise on Angling and Fly-Fishing and a Full Description of Tools, Tackle, and Implements* (Cincinnati: Robert Clarke & Co., 1881), 11–12.

33. Ibid., 155.

34. John Ortberg, *If You Want to Walk on Water, You've Got to Get Out of the Boat* (Grand Rapids, Mich.: Zondervan, 2000), 27–29.

35. Adapted from the *Los Angeles Times*, February 13, 1997.

36. Richard A. Swenson, M.D., *Margin: How to Create the Emotional, Physical, Financial and Time Reserves You Need* (Colorado Springs, Colo.: NavPress, 1992), 147.

37. Mark Domian Duda, "Degrees of Dedication—Who Fishes the Most and Why," *North American Fisherman*, Mar. 2001, 18, adapted.

38. *Webster's New World Dictionary* (New York: Prentice Hall, 1994), 1393.

39. Joe E. Brown, *Battle Fatigue* (Nashville, Tenn.: Broadman & Holman, 1995), adapted, 116–17.

40. Gord Pyzer, "For the Love of the Game, Curiosity Caught the Smallmouth," *In Fisherman*, Jan./Feb. 2001, 40–44, adapted.

41. Dr. Hal Schramm, "What Does Your Bass Really Weigh?" *North American Fisherman*, Mar. 2001, 37–42, adapted.

42. Bill Murphy and Paul Prorok, *In Pursuit of Giant Bass* (El Cajon, Calif.: Giant Bass Publishing), 88–93, adapted.

43. Drop-shot information adapted from numerous resources including *Bass West Magazine, In-Fisherman* magazine, and *North American Fisherman.*

44. James A. Garlow, *How God Saved Civilization* (Ventura, Calif.: Regal Books, 2000), 9.

45. Grigsby, 112–13, adapted.

46. Chuck Garrison, "Twenty Sure Ways to Lure Big Bass," *The Best of Bassmaster* (Montgomery, Ala.: Bass Anglers Sportsman Society of America, 1987), 320–21, adapted.

47. Ibid.

48. Grigsby.

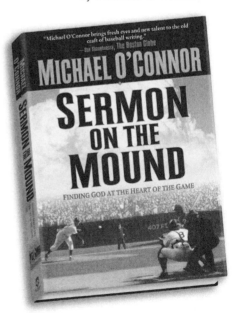